BETH FRANCIS

PROMISE OF SPRING

Complete and Unabridged

LINFORD
Leicester

First published in Great Britain in 2018

First Linford Edition
published 2021

*A catalogue record for this book is available
from the British Library.*

ISBN 978–1–4448–4572–3

Published by
Ulverscroft Limited
Anstey, Leicestershire

Set by Words & Graphics Ltd.
Anstey, Leicestershire
Printed and bound in Great Britain by
T J Books Ltd., Padstow, Cornwall

This book is printed on acid-free paper

1

Amy walked gingerly along the towpath, clinging onto the railings. Beside her, in its cast-iron channel, the dark water of the canal flowed slowly across the Dee Valley. Not usually nervous of heights, Amy had been surprised at her own queasiness. She lacked confidence in everything these days. It was time that changed.

She concentrated on a cluster of autumn leaves that had fallen in en route from Llangollen, trying to avoid looking at the sheer drop to the river below.

Her colleague Sally had shown her photographs of the Pontcysllte Aqueduct when they'd had a tea break during their night shift at the hospital.

'It's not far,' she'd teased Amy. 'I dare you to walk across. I was so scared when I went. Take a selfie to prove you've done it.'

She walked on towards the middle of the aqueduct, feeling braver with every step. Far below her she could hear the noise of the river as it tumbled swiftly towards Shropshire. She paused and stood looking out across the valley, watching birds flying between the branches of trees beneath her feet. People were jogging along the river bank, distance making them seem tiny. Horses galloped across a field, tossing their heads. The breeze blew her long chesnut hair across her face. She pushed it behind her ears, taking deep breaths of the clear air.

Over the past few months she'd gradually become used to working at a different hospital, but she hated her noisy, claustrophobic flat in town, and had just been to view a cottage in a nearby village. On her way back she'd passed the sign pointing to the aqueduct and, remembering Sally's teasing, had impulsively turned into the car park. But Sally's photographs hadn't prepared her for the breathtaking beauty of the view, or the peace of the surrounding countryside. This would be a good area to live. Not far to drive to the hospital, but a place where she could hibernate when she was off-duty.

A cyclist rode confidently past her, seemingly oblivious to the precipitous drop beneath his wheels. She watched as a narrowboat nosed onto the aqueduct and began its slow progress towards her. As it drew level, Amy smiled at the woman piloting the boat, and returned the waves of the passengers who were peering over the side, their faces a mixture of incredulity and panic.

She continued her walk, keeping pace with the barge, thinking about the cottage. Already knowing the property wouldn't be suitable, she'd followed the letting agent along a busy street, dodging early-morning shoppers. She'd clearly stated she wanted somewhere quiet.

Then the agent had turned into a gap between an antiques shop and a florist's, just wide enough to drive a car through.

The cobbled driveway led to a small courtyard, bounded by the high rear walls of the neglected gardens behind the shops and offices of the main street. Vivid, crimson-red leaves of Virginia creeper spilled over the bricks, adding a splash of autumn colour. To the left were two cottages. Tucked in behind the High Street, they looked ancient, remnants of a time before the car was invented and the shops were built.

One was obviously occupied. Tubs of white geraniums stood either side of a cheerful yellow front door. The second had a pile of empty recycling bins outside, and a 'To Let' sign in the window.

'What do you think?' the agent said, pushing the door open against a pile of circulars and uncollected mail. 'Convenient but quiet. Semi-detached, but the dividing walls are brick, not breezeblock and plaster. I know noise is a major concern for you. Each cottage has space to park one car. The shops, bus stop, even a leisure centre, are all within walking distance.

Amy stood on the step, listening. She could hardly hear the noise of the traffic; birds were screeching a warning as a tabby cat prowled along the top of the wall, but apart from that, silence.

Inside, the cosy living room and kitchen were ideal. The smaller of the two bedrooms had been converted into a bathroom, and the one remaining had views over the rooftops to the mountains. Amy told the agent she'd think about it and let her know, but her mind was made up.

She'd been so unhappy in her current flat, unable to sleep whatever shift she was on at the hospital, that she'd decided to leave within the first few weeks of moving in. When she was working nights, trying to sleep in the day, the walls vibrated with continuous rap music from one side. When she was working days, the frequent parties from the flat above kept her awake until the early hours. The neighbours were friendly and cheerful, and always invited her to join in the merriment, but that was little consolation as she struggled to get to know the staff and routines on her new ward with too little rest.

Her parents had been dubious when she'd phoned them to say she was thinking of moving out of the town into a small village.

'You won't get over Justin by hiding away,' her mother said, obviously convinced her daughter was broken-hearted.

Amy was annoyed. Why did her mother assume Justin had ended the romance?

'I'm not hiding away. I simply need somewhere quiet,' she'd insisted. 'You need somewhere you can make friends,' her mother continued.

'You need to meet new people.'

'I've met enough new people at work. What I need is to concentrate on my career,' she'd snapped, but then felt guilty. How could her mother understand how she was feeling when she hadn't told her the truth about her break-up with the man she'd thought she'd spend the rest of her life with? She hadn't told anyone

6

the truth. It was hard to admit, even to herself, how deeply she'd been taken in.

When Justin's apoplectic reaction to her decision to leave him forced her to move to a new town, she'd rented the first flat she'd looked at. Now she'd had time to look around, moving again would be a good thing, she was sure of it.

For the first time in many months she had something to look forward to. There was no need to delay. She reached for her mobile and phoned the agent.

She began the walk back across the aqueduct full of optimism. Leaving her previous job had been a wrench, but she was beginning to enjoy the challenge of her new post. She would make the cottage her home, and in her time off she'd walk along the many footpaths just a short distance from her front door.

She remembered her promise to take a photo for Sally and stood with her back to the railings, smiling self-consciously at the phone.

'Stunning view, isn't it?'

She'd been so engrossed she hadn't

noticed the man crouching down on the path, looking at some sort of black handle.

He looked up at her, grinning cheerfully, and she felt her pulse begin to race as his startlingly blue eyes met hers.

'I'd love to be here when they pull the plug out, wouldn't you?' he said, his voice warm and easy-going.

Amy was momentarily confused by her reaction. She had no intention of ever letting herself become attracted to anyone again, but it was hard not to respond to such open friendliness.

'Pull the plug out? You are joking?'

'Not at all. Every five years they close off the canal, open this valve and drain the water, so they can clean and maintain the trough. Fantastic piece of engineering.'

His enthusiasm was infectious and Amy was intrigued.

'The canal seems to be running along what looks like a wide tin bath, and now you're telling me it's got a plug. Are you sure it's safe?'

'It's been here for over two hundred years,' he said, getting to his feet.

'That's not reassuring.' Amy laughed nervously. Was it was the thought of rusty ironwork giving way beneath her, or the undisguised admiration in this undoubtedly attractive man's eyes, that was causing her concern?

'No need to worry; they knew what they were doing, those Victorian engineers,' he said.

He chatted enthusiastically about the canal and its construction as they both walked back across the aqueduct. By the time they reached the marina, her nervousness had faded. The sun was warm on her face as they stood for a few moments, watching the narrow-boats manoeuvring through the Trefor Basin. She felt relaxed, almost as if she were on holiday. It was a long time since she'd felt so comfortable in anyone's company.

'Have you time for coffee?' he asked.

She looked at her watch, and was dismayed to see how late it was. 'Sorry. I need to go. I'm working this evening,' she said.

As she hurried to her car, she knew that if she hadn't needed to rest before starting a night shift, she would have accepted the offer of coffee. And that would not have been a good idea. She might be feeling more optimistic, but she certainly had no wish to become involved in another relationship, however light-hearted.

Even so, she smiled as she started the engine and drove away. She didn't even know his name, but it had been good to talk to him.

2

As Amy returned to her car, Mike was overwhelmed by conflicting emotions. He only talked to her for a short while. They'd had a pleasant conversation. That was hardly enough reason for him to feel desolate, but he could barely stand to see her simply walk away.

He wanted to see her again, yet there was no way he could contact her.

He hadn't even asked her name! By the time he regained his senses and began to run after her, it was too late.

He watched as her car accelerated away and disappeared into the distance. There was nothing he could do. Shrugging his shoulders, he strolled across to the café, ordered coffee, and sat on a bench alone, watching the activity around the basin and trying to concentrate on why he was here.

It had been his great-aunt Meg's suggestion.

'Why don't you go for a walk along the towpath and across the aqueduct?' she'd said. 'It's a great place to think.'

He'd just told her he was considering applying for a job: project managing a major roadworks and canal renovation that was being planned at Betteley Locks. He'd left his flat in Sheffield very early in the morning and been to visit the site before driving on the extra thirty miles to see her. No wonder he suddenly felt so tired.

Aunt Meg had meant him to be thinking about the job, not about a girl he'd met halfway across the aqueduct.

'Tell me again, Mike,' she'd said. 'You're thinking of applying for a project to renovate a canal. Building locks, paddling about in mud. What happened to the work overseas? Tired of motorways and flyovers?'

'Not really. There's a flyover in this project. I'm tired of travelling,' he'd told her.

'And Emma?'

'You know we parted company, Aunt Meg,' he'd said. 'I told you months ago, when I phoned you on your birthday, remember?'

Mike smiled ruefully as he recalled the glare she'd given him. She was a feisty lady. Always had been.

'Of course I remember, Mike. I'm old, not stupid. But you've known Emma since you both started secondary school. You went to the same university. Stayed together since. I thought you'd probably just had an argument. I was quite pleased, to be honest. You've always been so placid, the pair of you. I thought a good old-fashioned row would shake you both out of your rut.'

Mike was startled into silence by her comments. He hadn't realised she had any concerns about his relationship with Emma.

She'd patted his arm. 'I'm sorry if you're upset, Mike. Do you want to talk about it, or shall we change the subject?'

Mike had realised he did want to talk

about his reaction to Emma's decision to suddenly break off their long relationship. His parents were being careful not to mention her, and his sister Lynda was too busy with her young family to do more than offer sympathy. Though she had started introducing him to her single girlfriends whenever he was home. It was very embarrassing.

Maybe Aunt Meg would understand. He'd always been able to talk to her.

It would be a relief to tell someone how he really felt.

'We didn't have an argument,' he said. 'Emma met someone else.'

'I always thought you would drift apart when you left university,' Aunt Meg said.

'I suppose we did, but neither of us realised it. We were both so busy we often didn't see each other for weeks at a time, but when we were together nothing seemed to have changed. Then Emma went to Lisbon on a weekend break, with a girlfriend. She met Eduardo and fell instantly in love. Her words, not mine. I don't believe in love at first sight.'

'It can happen, Mike.'

'I was working on a project in Germany at the time, and she flew over to tell me. She said she was giving up her career, and going to join him on his yacht.'

'That must have been very upsetting for you,' Aunt Meg sympathised.

'It should have been, shouldn't it?' Mike said. 'But to be honest, it wasn't. I was shocked, yes, but I was more demoralised than upset. I kept asking myself what Eduardo had that I didn't. Apart from his suave good looks and exotic lifestyle.'

He began pacing round the room.

'We'd known each other so long. It was always 'Mike and Emma'. We had the same group of friends, went to the same events. We stayed close when we started our jobs, even when we worked in different countries. I miss her company, but our relationship had been over for a long time. We'd both been too busy concentrating on our careers to notice. So, you see, I don't deserve sympathy.'

'You'd been together more from

habit than love,' Aunt Meg said. 'It isn't enough. As long as you're both happy...'

'I am now, and I assume Emma is,' Mike said. 'Though she knew nothing about this Eduardo. She didn't seem to know how he earned his money, but he had plenty of it. She hadn't met his family, but thought his parents lived in Lisbon. She knew he owned a villa and an expensive yacht, and she said she was madly in love with him.'

'Was it the money that attracted her?' Aunt Meg said.

'I'm sure not,' Mike said. 'Though the thought of sailing away and having an adventure might have appealed. It's different for me. I've been travelling around too much. I want to settle.'

'So you're thinking of a change of career?'

'It's not really a change. More of a sideways step. And I like the idea of moving back somewhere near here,' Mike said. 'I spent so much of my early childhood in the area. This job seems ideal. I've always been interested in this sort of work.'

'That's true,' his aunt agreed. 'Muddy puddles, just your thing. Always has been. And you were fascinated by the canal when you were a child. Remember the times we walked along the towpath? You should go for a short walk before you drive home. Clear your head.'

* * *

It had certainly been an eventful walk. He'd been standing on the bridge a while when the girl had stopped beside him. He'd already decided to apply for the job, and must have bored her as he chatted on about engineering work and the canal construction. No wonder she'd hurried away when he suggested coffee.

She hadn't seemed bored, though. He sighed as he recalled her ready smile, the laughter in her clear hazel eyes, the way she impatiently tucked her chestnut brown hair behind her ears every time the wind blew it across her face.

She had a sprinkle of freckles across

her nose...and he hadn't even asked her name.

Was this how Emma had felt when she met Eduardo? She hadn't watched him walk away with no idea if they would ever meet again. Suddenly her impetuous decision seemed sensible.

The girl's smiling face seemed imprinted on his brain. He tried to dismiss her from his mind as he drove back to Sheffield, but over the following weeks he couldn't get her out of his thoughts. She'd been hurrying off to work. She must live near the aqueduct. Maybe in Wrexham? How many people lived there? Sixty thousand? There was no chance he'd meet her again. He hadn't even asked her what her work was. He'd wasted his time prattling on about long-dead canal engineers.

3

A month later, Amy waved goodbye to the man-with-a-van and, despite the drizzle, stood for a moment gazing with satisfaction at her new home. Inside, all her possessions were piled in the living room, waiting on unpacking and sorting. It was a job she'd done many times before. Some of the boxes hadn't even been opened between her last few moves. This time would be different. She intended to make her home here.

'Hello. You must be my new neighbour.'

She hadn't heard anyone coming along the path, but turned to see an elderly lady, wearing a bright blue anorak, carrying a loaded shopping bag.

'I'm Meg Thomas. Welcome to Holly End.'

'Amy Weston,' Amy introduced herself.

'Come and have a cup of tea,' Meg offered. 'Any time. It'll be damp in there until you get the heating going.'

'Thanks,' Amy said, smiling as Mrs Thomas went into her own cottage. Meg Thomas had a kindly face. It looked as if she was about to make her first friend, though definitely not in the age range her mother had in mind.

The cottage was chilly: it had rained on and off for the last few weeks, and the previous tenants had moved out several months ago. Best to get the heating going before starting the unpacking. She headed for the cupboard housing the boiler, armed with the instructions that had been left conspicuously on the kitchen work surface. Fortunately, there were no problems, and the radiators were soon warming. She began moving boxes, concentrating on finding those labelled 'Bedroom' and 'Kitchen'. As long as she could sleep in a warm bed and make a meal tonight, the bulk of the work could be done tomorrow.

By the time she located her bedding

and lugged it upstairs, she was warm enough; too hot, really. She systematically checked the radiators and set them on low before making her bed, then, seeing the rain had stopped, opened the sash window, and stood for a while watching the clouds race across the skyline. In spite of the negativity from her family, she was certain this was going to be a good move.

Back downstairs she began emptying the box containing her emergency kitchen equipment: kettle, mugs, teabags, milk and biscuits. She ran the water for a while before filling the kettle and plugging it in. As she waited for it to boil, her mobile rang.

'Hi, Mum.'

'How's it going, love? Did the van come?'

'Yes, Mum. All done. He unloaded and went a few hours ago. I'm just about to have a drink.'

'Oh, good. Then we can have a little chat. I do worry about you, Amy. I wish you had let us come to help … '

'I know you worry about me, Mum, and I wish you'd stop. It's too far for you to drive down here from the Lake District just to help move boxes. Come when I've got the cottage looking homely. You and Dad could stay for a few nights, though I'd have to sleep on the sofa - there's only one bedroom.'

'That would be nice. I hope you won't be lonely.'

'I'll be revelling in the quiet. At least I should be able to sleep tonight.'

'You know what I mean, love. You'll have no friends close by. It might be ages before you meet anyone.'

'I've already met my neighbour,' Amy contradicted her, remembering Mrs Thomas's offer. 'She's invited me round for a mug of tea.'

'Oh that's good news. A friend. What does she do?'

Amy grinned. Mrs Thomas must be at least eighty, but her mother would already be imagining shopping trips, invitations to parties, and possibly introductions to unattached brothers.

'No idea, Mum. I'm about to find out. I'll speak to you tomorrow.'

Amy switched her own kettle off, locked her front door and went to knock on her neighbour's, hoping the invitation had been genuine and not simply a moment of unguarded politeness, instantly regretted.

Mrs Thomas was delighted to see her and bustled around making the tea and cutting slices of lemon cake.

'You'll need to keep your strength up,' she insisted as Amy protested at the size of the portion she was given. 'Moving house is hard work. Took me months to get sorted when I moved in here. I've still got boxes unopened in the spare bedroom.'

'How long have you been living here, Mrs Thomas?'

'Call me Meg. Everyone else does. I've only been in this cottage a few years, but I've lived in the area all my life. Anything you need to know, just ask.'

Time passed quickly as Meg told her where all the best shops were, that there was a swimming pool at the leisure centre, the nearest way to the footpath along the river.

Her new neighbour was not only knowledgeable, she was fun. She'd walked the local mountain paths all her life and said she still went out walking every week with a group of friends.

They chatted about Amy's plans to turn the tiny yard behind her cottage into a patio filled with pots of flowers and herbs, and Meg offered to help with plants and cuttings.

As Amy stood to leave she paused to look at the photographs on the sideboard.

'That's Hugo, my husband,' Meg said. 'He died many years ago. The photo next to him is my sister, Lily.'

'She looks like you. Does she live nearby?'

'Not any longer. She's in Sheffield, with her daughter Gwen. She came to live with me after she was widowed. I had a big house then, and a huge garden. We'd always got on well, and we had a few happy years before she became frail and ill, and Gwen took her back to live with her.'

'You must have missed her.'

'I did, but Lily needed a lot of care, so I suppose it was for the best. My niece thought I would be lonely and wanted me to sell up and move near her. She said the house was too big for me, that soon I wouldn't be able to manage the distance to the shops, or cope with the garden.'

'You weren't tempted to go?'

'No. I didn't want to leave the village. But Gwen was right in many ways: my house was too big. When I saw this cottage for sale I moved, while I still had the energy to do so.'

Meg picked up a photograph of a young woman holding a baby, with a toddler by her side.

'That's Gwen, with her children Mike and Lynda. She's such a kind girl, Gwen, but a non-stop worrier. Takes on everyone's problems. I don't tell her half the things I do.

'Here's Mike grown up, playing with Lynda's son,' Meg said, pointing to another photo. 'He always keeps in touch. Came for a brief visit when he was in the area a few weeks ago.'

It was a good photo. Amy recognised him instantly. That cheerful, open face was hard to forget. Over the past weeks she'd remembered their chance meeting at the aqueduct, and alternately regretted having to leave so quickly, and been relieved that she had. If he came to visit his great-aunt there was a possibility they'd meet again. Her head hoped not, but she felt a tingle of anticipation at the thought.

She looked more closely at the picture. Mike was laughing merrily, his eyes full of mischief as he kicked a beachball with the toddler. A woman was standing in the background, looking bored.

'Is that Lynda?' she asked.

'No. That's Emma. Mike's friend.' Meg's voice was cool, almost disapproving.

Amy sighed. He was clearly in a relationship. Why wouldn't he be? His offer of coffee had obviously been just that. It was fortunate she had needed to go to work. She must have imagined the admiration in his eyes. She shouldn't need reminding there was something seriously wrong where her judgement of men was concerned. It was best to avoid them all.

4

When Meg Thomas left the leisure centre after her swim, the wind was blowing strongly across the car park, bringing a chill edge to the early morning. But in spite of the wind, the sun was shining, and she decided to spend the rest of the day working on her allotment. There were vegetables to be harvested, but the gardening year was winding down. She wanted to start preparing the ground ready for the rush of planting in the spring.

She didn't see the discarded plastic bag blowing along in the wind. It wrapped itself round her ankle and she tripped, falling heavily on the arm she stretched out to save herself.

The pain was excruciating. Briefly, she lay where she had fallen, moaning quietly, but hearing footsteps approaching, she struggled to sit up. She didn't want anyone making a fuss. She needed to get home, but the pain was too much, and she collapsed back onto the paving slabs, her eyes closed, waiting for it to subside.

'Are you all right, dear?'

'She's unconscious. Better call an ambulance.'

'She was just walking along and fell, poor thing.'

A few moments ago there had been no-one around; now Meg shuddered as she realised she was the centre of attention.

'I'm not unconscious. I've just hurt my arm,' she said.

'Is there someone we can phone, dear?'

'Can you sit up?'

'She's shivering.'

The voices swirled round as Meg fought against the pain. Then, suddenly, a voice she recognised.

'Meg. Meg, it's Amy. Remember? Your new neighbour.'

'Of course I remember. I've hurt my arm, not my head,' Meg grumbled.

'What are you doing here?'

'Going to the gym before I go home to bed,' Amy said.

'Oh, good. Someone you know. Hope you soon recover, dear.'

'Must get off to work. I'll be late.'

'I must go, but I've phoned for an ambulance. It shouldn't be long.'

Meg heard the group that had gathered around make their excuses and drift away as Amy knelt down beside her.

She struggled to sit up. 'Sorry I'm so crotchety, Amy. I think I've broken my arm. I must have tripped over something.'

'Pain can make anyone short-tempered,' Amy said. 'The ambulance should be here soon. I'll come to the hospital with you.'

'No, you've only just left there. Go home and sleep.'

'I'm not leaving you sitting on the pavement shivering. I'll fetch a blanket from my car.'

'You go home,' Meg repeated when Amy returned with the blanket, but she was unable to suppress a moan.

'We'll see what the paramedics say. Is there someone you want me to call to let them know where you are?'

'I don't think so. I wasn't meeting anyone today.'

'Relatives? Your niece?'

Meg tensed. She didn't want Gwen driving over in a panic, insisting on taking her back to Sheffield. She was already close to breaking point looking after Lily. She didn't need more stress.

'Don't tell her, Amy. Please. She doesn't know I go swimming. I'll be fine once I've had my arm set.'

There was no mistaking the look Amy gave her. They both knew she wouldn't be fine. Apart from the pain, if her arm was broken, it was going to be very difficult to manage to do even basic things for the next few weeks.

'I'll ring Gwen later,' Meg promised. 'Once I've had my arm attended to. You need to rest. You've been working all night. Go home as soon as the ambulance comes.'

Before Amy could reply, the ambulance pulled into the car park and the paramedics took over. Meg answered their questions firmly, very clear about what had happened, and what she thought needed doing. She managed to stand and say goodbye to Amy as she was helped towards the ambulance.

'I'll let you know when I'm home,' she said. 'It'll be hours, I expect.'

'I'll go home, but only if you promise to phone me when you're ready to leave the hospital. I'll come and fetch you. Have you got a mobile?'

'Of course I've got a mobile,' Meg grumbled. 'In my handbag. Where's my handbag?'

'Here,' the paramedic said. 'Don't worry, we picked it up for you.'

'Can I look for your phone, Meg?' Amy asked. 'I'll put my number in for you.'

'I don't want to be a nuisance,' Meg fretted. 'I can wait for an ambulance to take me home.'

'No need,' Amy insisted. 'Besides,

they mightn't let you go home unless they know there's someone to help you. I can make sure the house is warm and get some food for you.'

Meg was settled in the ambulance, the doors were shut, and they began the drive to the hospital before she could protest further. She was feeling dizzy and sick now, but once she'd been X-rayed and had her arm set, she was sure she'd feel better.

She would need to feel calmer before phoning Gwen. Whatever happened, she was determined not to be taken to Sheffield. Her niece was already caring for Lily, and had enough to do without someone else to look after.

'I can manage,' she said as they arrived at the hospital and the paramedics helped her from the ambulance. But her legs were so unsteady that she was forced to accept being gently settled in a chair and wheeled into the Accident and Emergency department.

Her agitation increased as a nurse began to take her details: noting her age, asking if she lived alone and was there anyone at home to look after her? She didn't want to stay in hospital a minute longer than necessary. It would be easy to cook simple meals one-handed. It wouldn't hurt to have egg on toast for a while, instead of a cooked dinner. And she had several friends who would call to see her, and bring fresh milk and bread, until she felt a bit less shaky.

She didn't want to impose on Amy. It wasn't fair. She hardly knew her, but telling the nurse that her next-door neighbour was also a nurse, and would collect her when she was ready to leave, seemed the quickest way to get home without causing everyone a lot of needless trouble.

5

Amy watched the ambulance go, gave up her plan to spend an hour in the gym, and returned home, her thoughts turning to a snack, a shower, then bed. It had been a long night with a few very sick patients, and an admission towards morning. She'd been relieved to hand over at the end of the shift, knowing she had a few days off.

She'd not been expecting to drive back to the hospital today, but if Meg were allowed home she would certainly need some support. She would be in shock after her fall. Amy was happy to help until she went back to work, but then Meg would be on her own. Maybe by tomorrow she'd be less reluctant to phone her niece.

As she settled to sleep, Amy wondered whether Mike would come, if his mother couldn't. The thought of him staying in the next-door cottage, looking after his great-aunt, was strangely comforting. She would see him when she came home from work. Could offer to help. They would get to know each other. Half-asleep, she indulged herself in a daydream where Mike and she were laughing together, where he leaned forward to kiss her ... No! She sat up and plumped the pillows furiously.

If he did come, it would be for a short visit. Presumably he had a job to go to. He wouldn't remember her. Why would he? She would have slipped from his mind the moment she left him at the aqueduct. He would have sat drinking his coffee, thinking about that girl in the photograph. What was her name? Emma. That was it.

She needed to sleep. What was she doing wasting time thinking about Mike? Even if Emma was no more than a casual friend, it made no difference. She would never become involved in another relationship. Justin had been a very plausible liar. She'd had no idea of the double life he'd led, or of the vicious temper under-lying his genial personality. She would not risk being taken in again.

She didn't need anyone. She could make a life on her own. She lay back down and resolutely turned her thoughts to her childhood. Summer days helping her grandfather on his allotment, when the biggest problem was which plant was a weed and which would grow into a carrot or a lettuce. A time when she went to bed in the evening, slept, and woke refreshed next morning. Not as now, when she struggled to sleep during the day and worked a twelve-hour shift through the night. She often woke as tired as when she went to bed.

Eventually she did sleep, but her rest was disturbed by nightmares. She could close her mind to thoughts of Justin when she was awake, but his charming face transformed by anger still invaded her dreams, chasing after her, screaming threats.

It was a relief when the phone rang,

jolting her back to the present, and problems she could deal with.

'I'm sorry to be such a nuisance,' Meg said. 'But could you possibly come and fetch me?'

'Of course. I'll be straight there,' Amy said, already starting to pull her clothes towards her.

★ ★ ★

'Hi Amy,' Meg greeted her cheerfully. 'I'm so sorry to bother you.'

Amy was relieved to see that her neighbour, though frail and ill, was looking much better than she had been when she'd been helped into the ambulance.

The nurse looking after her came over. 'Hello. Amy, isn't it? I've seen you a few times around the hospital. Mrs Thomas told us all about you. She says you're a great neighbour. She thinks the world of you.'

Amy chuckled. She had immediately liked her sprightly neighbour, but their shared tea and cake on the day she'd

38

moved in was hardly enough for Meg to 'think the world of her'. She had obviously exaggerated their relationship to get home.

'Mrs Thomas will need a bit of help,' the nurse continued. Meg was looking at her steadily, pleading almost.

Thinking Meg would probably recover quicker in her own home than on a noisy hospital ward, Amy grinned at her.

'Come on, then.' She helped Meg up off the chair. 'Home it is. You'll be ready for a cup of tea, no doubt.'

'They don't always plaster broken bones any more,' Meg said as they walked slowly to the car. 'Look. They've put it in this splint thing. Fortunately it's my left arm. I'll be able to manage most things, and I went shopping yesterday, so I've plenty of food in.'

'Why don't you phone your niece and go to stay with her for a few weeks?' Amy suggested.

'She's got enough to do looking after Lily. She'll go into a flap, drive straight over and insist on wrapping me up in cotton wool. I can just see her face if I tell her I fell coming out of the gym.'

'So you're still determined to manage on your own?'

'I am. I can't expect Gwen to look after me when I refuse to go and live near her. It doesn't seem fair.'

'But you should tell her,' Amy said. 'She's your closest relative, and she obviously cares a lot about you.'

'I will,' Meg promised. 'I'll drop it into the conversation when she phones next. Hopefully it won't be for a few days, and I'll be able to tell her how well I'm coping.'

'It's fortunate I've got a few days off, then, isn't it?' Amy said. 'I'll get you something to eat once we're home, and see what else you need doing.'

'You don't want to be spending your time running around after me. I only said you'd help me so they would let me come home. You'll have things you want to do. People you want to go out with. Young people.'

'Not really, to be honest. I don't

know anyone locally. I'll be glad of the company.'

Amy was trying to reassure Meg, but was speaking the truth. She didn't have anything planned.

Once they reached home she could see Meg needed to rest, so she helped her settle, then left her to sleep, promising to come back in a few hours and prepare a meal. Subdued now, Meg gave her the spare key to let herself in, and Amy went back to her own cottage, still concerned about her neighbour. While she admired her spirit, and respected her wish to be independent, she thought Meg was seriously underestimating the difficulty she would have over the next few weeks, even if there were no complications.

Any attempt to try to organise her life would be met by strong resistance, but she would try to persuade her to phone her niece. It sounded as if Gwen kept in constant touch, though their conversations seemed to leave a lot out, with Meg only telling Gwen things she would approve of. Gwen didn't know about the swimming. What else didn't she know?

The phone ringing interrupted her thoughts.

'You said you'd ring when you woke up today,' her mother said. 'Did you forget?'

'Sorry, Mum. I've been next door with my neighbour – she ...'

'Oh, yes. Your neighbour. You were going to have tea with her the day you moved in. What did you say her name was?'

'Meg. Meg Thomas. She's broken her arm. I've just been to fetch her home from hospital. That's why I forgot to phone.'

'How did she break her arm?'

'She fell, coming out of the leisure centre after going swimming. I've started going there for half an hour when I come off night shift. When I arrived she was lying on the pavement.'

'Oh dear. Poor Meg. I'm so relieved you've made a friend. Not that Meg will be able to go to the gym with you for several weeks.'

'No. But knowing her, she'll be wanting to go for long walks,' Amy sighed, thinking Meg would soon begin to feel confined. She was evidently used to getting out and about.

'You'll be able to go with her, Amy,' her mother said cheerfully.

Amy laughed, but didn't explain that Meg was old enough to be her grandmother. She was being as evasive with her mother as Meg was with her niece. There might be over half a century between them in age, but they were both trying to stop their relatives worrying about them.

6

'I really think you should tell your niece about your accident,' Amy said when she visited Meg the following morning and found her slumped in a chair, exhausted by the effort of getting up and dressed.

'She'll worry,' Meg fretted.

'How would you feel if she was ill and didn't tell you?'

'I'm not ill. I broke my arm.'

'I'll make you a cup of tea. Then what would you like for breakfast?' Arny asked, deciding to change the subject for a while.

'Porridge, please.' Meg sighed. 'I did manage to make tea, but I'd love another cup. Are you going to eat with me?'

'I am. I haven't had porridge for ages. Real comfort food. Shall we have toast with it?'

By the time they'd finished breakfast, Meg was looking much better.

44

'I think I feel calm enough to speak to Gwen now,' she said. 'You are right, Amy. It's only fair to tell her.'

Amy took the dishes to the kitchen, while Meg talked to her niece, but she was soon called back into the living room.

'Amy, can you talk to Gwen? She doesn't believe me when I say I can manage.'

Reluctantly, Amy took the phone and introduced herself, before being bombarded by a stream of anxious worries and queries while Meg hovered in the background.

'I can see it's impossible for you to come,' Amy said, when she eventually managed to speak. 'You've enough to cope with there.' Meg nodded in agreement.

'Yes, I know it takes longer to recover once you're elderly, but your aunt seems very fit for her age, and determined.'

Amy laughed as Gwen described just how determined her aunt could be. 'I think the best thing is for me to get

George – that's my husband – to come over at the weekend and bring Aunt Meg back here where I can look after her. I really can't get there sooner,' Gwen said.

'I can help out,' Amy reassured her. 'I'm off work for a few days, so I'll be available while Mrs Thomas gets over the shock. After that, I can call in before I go to work in the evening, and when I get home in the morning.'

'You work nights?'

'Yes. I'm a nurse at the local hospital.'

'Oh, I didn't realise. What a relief. It's so kind of you.'

'I'll give your aunt as much help as she needs. Or is prepared to accept,' Amy added, seeing the mutinous look on Meg's face.

'Tell Aunt Meg George will come to fetch her on Saturday. She can stay here until her arm is better. We'll use the time she's here to persuade her to sell that cottage and come to live near us, but don't tell her that. There's a retirement flat for sale nearby. It's on the third floor, but there are lifts.'

'What's she been saying?' Meg asked as Amy finished the call.

'She sounds very concerned about you,' Amy prevaricated, knowing Meg would not be pleased by the turn the conversation had taken.

'She is. She's a lovely girl.' Meg sighed. 'She means well.'

'She says her husband will come at the weekend and take you to stay with them until your arm's better.'

'We'll see about that. I'll phone her back. She's got enough to do looking after Lily. I'll visit when I'm better and can help her out a bit. Silly girl. Always trying to do too much.'

'If you won't go to Sheffield, you'll have to let me help you,' Amy said.

'You are helping me, and in a few days I'll be able to get around more. My friend, Madge will bring me any shopping I need. You'll have enough to do.'

'To be honest, I'm a bit lonely,' Amy said. 'If you let me cook your meals, we could eat together and you can talk to me. You can tell me all about the village.'

'It's a shame to be buying vegetables when mine are just waiting to be picked,' Meg said that evening as they ate dinner. 'I should be getting on with things. The weeds will be smothering everything. Never let a weed … '

' … see a Sunday,' Amy finished. 'My Granddad used to say that. He said if you pull the weeds before they have chance to set seed, you save yourself seven years' weeding.'

'Sensible man, your Granddad.'

'He was. He died a few years ago, and I still miss him. I spent hours with him when I was small, helping on his allotment.'

'Mike used to help me in my garden,' Meg said. 'His sister wasn't interested, but Mike would trundle up and down with his wheelbarrow, or hoe between the plants. Never happier than when he had his red wellies on and could get muddy. Hardly surprising that he patters around in the mud now, doing engineering projects.'

Amy glanced at the photograph of Mike. It was easy to imagine him striding along muddy paths. She struggled to dismiss the thought.

'Where do you grow vegetables? I've only got a small yard behind my cottage. There's barely enough room for a rotary clothes line.'

'Same here,' Meg said. 'I have a tiny patio with a few pots of bulbs. I had a huge garden at my old house. It was too much to manage, really.'

'So you downsized?'

'I did. Gwen was pleased. She said if I was too stubborn to move to live near her, and wouldn't even consider a retirement flat, then this cottage was the next best thing. In many ways it's perfect for me. I have more time to see my friends and I like the convenience, but I've always grown my own fruit and vegetables. That's why I... You won't tell Gwen, will you?'

'Won't tell Gwen what? What have you been up to?'

'I've got an allotment,' Meg said. 'I go most days, weather permitting.'

'Why shouldn't I tell Gwen? I think it's a lovely idea.'

'She'd not be best pleased. She was so relieved when I sold my house and moved here. She said she wouldn't have to worry about me being out gardening in all sorts of weather, risking hurting myself, or catching pneumonia. She thinks I should take more care. Sit in a chair and do my knitting.'

'Nothing wrong with knitting,' Amy said. 'I knit, and crochet. It's trendy these days.'

'I can't knit with my arm like this, even if I wanted to,' Meg fretted. 'Besides, it's my vegetables I'm worried about. The place will be looking such a mess. It'll be ages before I'll be able to do anything useful.'

Amy sympathised. She remembered her grandfather working hard on his allotment in the autumn, preparing the ground for the next year's planting. Meg was going to have to leave it this year, unless she knew anyone locally who could help out.

'I was thinking…when are you back at work, Amy?' Meg asked.

'Not until Sunday evening. Is there something you need me to do?'

'Would you walk along to my allotment? Just have a look to see how things are?'

'I'd love to. I'll go the first dry day we have,' Amy promised.

'You could bring vegetables back. There should be carrots, and a few onions, and maybe cabbages. And could you go in the shed, and bring me my tin of seeds? I could sort those out while I'm stuck here. I could make a list of what I need to order for next year.'

'If your niece finds out about the allotment she may try to persuade you to give it up before next year,' Amy said.

'Then we won't tell her, will we?'

Meg winked, and in spite of her misgivings, Amy laughed. While talking about her gardening, Meg looked more animated than she had all day. Her relationship with her niece was her own business.

7

Mike had almost given up hope of hearing from the company he'd applied to, about the engineering project at Betteley Locks, when he received an email inviting him for an interview the following Monday.

He decided to drive over a day early and have another look at the site before booking into a hotel in Manchester, where the interview was to be held. He sat at his desk reviewing all the information he'd been sent, then researching similar projects, making sure he could answer any questions the interview panel threw at him.

He knew he could take on this work and do it well. He would have excellent references from his previous work. He wasn't going to let lack of preparation stop him presenting a good case for them to employ him.

'Your Aunt Meg's broken her arm,' his mother told him, when he called in to visit his parents, a few days later.

'What happened? Did she stumble? Those cobblestones can be slippery in the wet.'

'I didn't ask how she did it.' Gwen frowned. 'I spoke mainly to her neighbour.'

'Her neighbour? Someone must have moved into the cottage next door. It was empty when I last visited.'

'You didn't tell me she was living next to an empty property.'

'I didn't tell you because you'd have become agitated about Aunt Meg being isolated. The cottage has been empty since the owners went abroad. They were coming back, but they've decided to stay in France and let the cottage.

When I was there Aunt Meg said the agent had shown a few people around, so I didn't think it would be empty long.'

'I'd still like to have known,' Gwen said. 'Aunt Meg could have fallen and lain for days with no-one next door to hear, even if she hammered on the wall.'

Mike sighed. It was hard deciding what to tell his mother and what to keep quiet about. She had always been a worrier, seeing danger at every turn, but she fretted about things even more since his grandmother had come to live with her.

'That's unlikely, Mum,' he said. 'If Aunt Meg wasn't well, she would phone someone. She always has her mobile nearby. And she has a busy social life. Even if she couldn't phone, one of her friends would soon realise she needed help. You said you spoke to the new neighbour?'

'I did. She sounded very nice. Apparently she's a nurse and has a few days off, so is happy to help for now. I said your father would go and fetch Aunt Meg this weekend, but she's just rung back insisting she can manage.'

'That sounds like Aunt Meg,' Mike said. 'Independent.'

'Stubborn,' Gwen said. 'I don't know what to do. She simply won't act her age, that's her problem.'

Mike laughed. 'She never will.'

'It's not funny, Mike. I'm really worried, and I can't leave your grandmother. How was Aunt Meg when you saw her?'

'Fit and well,' Mike said. 'She'd just come back from a walk with friends.'

He watched as his mother paced anxiously up and down the kitchen. She was exhausted. His grandmother Lily needed more and more care. His father helped, and he and Lynda did what they could, but the main burden fell on his mother.

'Try not to fret, Mum,' he said.

'Bones don't heal quickly at her age. And she'll be trying to do things too soon and fall over again.'

'I'll go to see how she's coping,' Mike said. 'I came to tell you I've heard from that job I applied for. I'm going to Betteley Locks at the weekend, so I could easily go across to Hen Bont to visit Aunt Meg.'

'Oh Mike, would you? Maybe you could persuade her to reconsider. She'll listen to you.'

'Aunt Meg won't listen to anyone.

Remember, we used to have huge arguments when I was growing up, though we always ended up laughing.'

'You could both be so stubborn. You're very similar in many ways. She used to enjoy having what she called 'an exchange of views' with you.'

Mike grinned, remembering summer holidays when he'd tried to persuade Aunt Meg he was allowed to do things she knew his mother forbade. They could scrap for hours and still remain friends. His grandparents, Lily and Harold, had lived nearby, but were often away. It was Aunt Meg he and Lynda had stayed with more often. She'd taught them to swim, taken them cycling, let them put up tents in the garden, played cricket and football with them. He'd do anything he could to make sure she was contented and safe. He loved her dearly.

'I'll go on Sunday. If she needs looking after, I'll try to persuade her to let me go back after my interview and bring her here. But I don't think she'll change her mind. She's comfortable in her cottage and there's always someone coming to see her. Madge and Emrys call in often.'

'I'd forgotten them. They've been friends with Aunt Meg for years. Their son Dafydd's the same age as me. We learnt to swim together.'

'She knows so many people. Unless she's feeling really ill, she'll want to stay where she is. But if I'm really concerned about her, I'll insist on bringing her back with me. No matter how much she objects.'

★ ★ ★

Mike left Sheffield very early on Sunday morning. He parked in Betteley Marsh, the nearest village to the project, and despite the rain, walked to the site along the overgrown towpath beside the disused waterway.

He remembered, from his previous visit, that the canal beyond the derelict locks had already been brought back into use. Plans to construct a new bridge to upgrade the road over the canal included the complete reconstruction of the flight of three locks. It was a complicated project, but well within his capabilities.

Brambles and nettles almost obliterated the path in places, but as he pushed his way through, and neared the broken lock gates, he could visualise the area in a few years' time. Once the construction work was finished and the site handed over, a team of volunteers would take over bringing this derelict stretch of waterway back into use. It would become busy again: people would bring their families to walk along the towpath, and narrowboats would be able to travel to Betteley Marsh and turn in the restored marina. It would be like the stretch of canal from the aqueduct to Llangollen.

The aqueduct. He couldn't think of it without remembering the girl he'd met the last time he had walked there. He could see her as clearly as if she were standing in front of him. If he closed his eyes he could almost hear her voice.

She was never far from his mind. How was it possible for such a brief meeting to have become imprinted on his brain so vividly?

Resolutely, he pushed the image away as he tried to concentrate on familiarising himself with the site.

8

Meg was delighted when Madge and Emrys knocked on her door on Sunday morning. The early-morning rain had cleared, the sun was shining, and she was feeling confined.

It had rained most of the week, so when Amy had seen the clouds roll away and decided to go to the allotment, Meg had wanted to walk with her.

'There's a footpath by the river,' she said. 'It's not far.'

Amy thought the path might be slippery with mud, and that it was too soon after her accident.

Meg hadn't objected. She knew Amy planned to have an early lunch, then try to rest before starting the night shift. She would need to walk briskly; she wouldn't want to be slowed down by a doddery old lady.

'We've brought you the latest gardening magazine,' Madge said. 'And cake.'

'You don't know how pleased I am to see you,' Meg said. 'Come in. I'll put the kettle on.'

'I'll do it,' Emrys said. 'You chat to Madge. You must be feeling really fed up.'

'I am,' Meg agreed. 'One moment's carelessness and six whole weeks out of action.'

'Sorry we didn't come before, but we've only just got home from Dafydd's. We heard you'd had an accident, when we were buying our paper. How are you managing? Is your arm painful?'

'It's not too bad,' Meg said. 'But it does ache. I don't think I'll be able to come on the walk this week. Nothing wrong with my legs, but my balance isn't good with one arm out of use. And I'm so tired all the time.'

'You will be tired. It's the shock. I was ages getting back to normal when I broke my leg last year. Remember?' Madge said. 'What does your Gwen say about it?'

'You know Gwen. She's upset. Wants to wrap me in cotton wool. She'd be shocked if she knew I fell after going swimming.'

'Maybe not,' Madge said. 'I remember you teaching Gwen to swim years ago. Lily and Harold had gone abroad somewhere and left her with you. It rained most of the time and we spent hours at the swimming pool, me and my Dafydd, you and Gwen.'

'I remember.' Meg smiled. 'Gwen was so proud of herself. Lily would never have taught her. My sister liked her water warm and soapy.'

'You were like a second mother to Gwen,' Emrys said, as he brought the tea and cake in on a tray. 'No wonder she worries about you.'

'How is Lily? Any improvement?' Madge asked.

'No, she's steadily deteriorating. It's heartbreaking for Gwen. She says sometimes her mother doesn't even recognise her.'

She sipped her tea, thinking about her

niece. She'd been a quiet child. She'd come to stay often when her parents were away. They'd done a lot together: walking, swimming, even horse-riding. When her own children were growing up, Gwen had been happy for Mike and Lynda to come to stay with her during their school holidays.

'Gwen has worried about me, ever since Lily went to live with her,' she said. 'When she phones she's always telling me what I should or shouldn't do. It's easier not to mention things she may disapprove of.'

'Like what?' Madge asked.

'Well, swimming, for one thing. Though, as you say, she may not mind that. And she doesn't know about our walking group.'

'But we've all been walking for years,' Emrys said.

'Yes, she knows we go for walks, but she thinks it's gentle strolls along the river bank. She'd be horrified if she knew we still went for long walks in the mountains. Does your Dafydd know?'

'Of course he does,' Madge said. 'He boasts to all his friends that we can walk as far as him.'

'Gwen's different. She would say I might fall, I must be careful, I should remember my age. I know she's concerned, but I'm not ready to give up yet. When I told her about my accident she wanted to send George to fetch me, but fortunately my new neighbour was here and she told Gwen she'd help me for a bit.'

'Oh, someone's moved in next door. That's good. What's she like?' Madge asked.

'Lovely young girl. Nurse at the hospital. She's been coming and cooking a meal each day, and we eat it together. I feel dreadful imposing on her like this. She says she doesn't know anyone around here and is glad of the company, but I think she's just being kind.'

'We'll have to introduce her to some locals,' Emrys said.

'Who do we know who's under sixty-five, Emrys?' Madge said. 'She'll hardly want to spend all her free time with people old enough to be her grand-parents.'

'She's gone along to my allotment this morning,' Meg said. 'That's another thing I haven't told Gwen about. She thinks gardening is too much for me.'

When they left, promising to call in again next day, Meg picked up the magazine they'd brought, scowling with annoyance as she read an article listing all the things she should be doing in her garden in October. She knew exactly what she should be doing: harvesting, hoeing, clearing the ground of this year's crops and preparing the soil ready for next year. She always tidied her shed and cleaned her garden tools in November. Surely her arm would be completely healed by then?

She threw the magazine onto the coffee table, and sat thinking about Amy. The girl needed to be making friends her own age. Was there anyone at the allotments she might meet?

There was Bill Williams, at plot five.

He'd chat to anyone. But he was ancient, and Fred, who tended the patch next to hers, was well past retirement age. There were the three girls who had taken a plot between them. She remembered the day they'd arrived, full of enthusiasm and laughter, determined to grow all their own vegetables and be self-sufficient. They'd stuck at it, too.

Making up with effort what they lacked in expertise, bringing their young children with them, livening up the whole site with peals of laughter. If they were there this morning, they'd soon make Amy welcome.

Pity Mike lived so far away! If he got the job he'd been interested in, she could introduce them when he came to visit. Had Gwen told him about her accident? If so, he'd phone. She'd find it harder to fool Mike than anyone else. He would be able to tell straight away that she was feeling low.

9

...

Amy had enjoyed the walk along the river-
bank to the allotments. The main access
was from a lane off the High Street, but
Meg had told her there was a small gate
onto the footpath at the bottom of the
site. She found it easily, pushed it open,
and paused to look around.

She took a deep breath, enjoying the
smell of damp earth. It took her right back
to her childhood, when she'd helped her
grandfather work on his patch. Some of
her happiest times had been spent with
him.

A few people were already busy harvesting. They raised a hand in greeting
as she passed, watching curiously as
she continued on, past plot after plot,
towards the top of the field, where Meg
had said hers was.

Granddad's plot had been on a site
much the same as this, though the views

hadn't been so magnificent. The ground sloped away towards the river, and in the background were the mountains, moving in and out of visibility as the wind chased the clouds across the peaks. They seemed tantalisingly close. Amy promised herself walks in those mountains before winter closed in.

She began to inspect the neat rows of vegetables, pulling handfuls of weeds out as she went. It was only when she inadvertently pulled out a nettle, and picked a dock leaf to wrap round her stinging hand, that she recalled Meg's list and remembered this was only to be a quick visit.

She went to the wooden shed in search of something with which to dig up the carrots. The door creaked on rusty hinges as she turned the key and pulled it open. Inside, the shelves were crammed with tools, tins and boxes. She soon located a garden fork, and the biscuit tin containing the seeds. Then she spotted a fold-up chair. If she drove here on her next day off, Meg could come with her.

She could sit in the chair, with a blanket for warmth, and say what she wanted done. Between them they should be able to keep the plot tidy until the end of the season.

She was busy digging carrots and potatoes and shaking the soil off before putting them in the basket, when she heard a shout.

'Hey! What are you doing? They're not your vegetables.'

She'd been so preoccupied she'd not noticed the elderly man walking up the path. Now she stood clutching a bunch of freshly pulled carrots, feeling as guilty as if she really had been stealing them.

'I know,' she stuttered. 'Mrs Thomas asked me to fetch them for her.'

'Sorry, I didn't mean to shout.' The man looked less fierce as he came nearer. He reminded her of her grandfather, with his weather-beaten face crinkling into a welcoming smile. 'I thought you were one of those young hooligans. We've had a bit of trouble lately with vandalism, and we try to look out for each other.

I haven't seen Meg all week. Is she all right?'

Amy explained about Meg's accident.

'I'm sorry about that. Tell her Bill was asking after her, won't you? And if there's anything I can do to help, let me know. I'm sure I'll see you again if you're going to be helping out,' he said as he ambled off.

Amy was chuckling at the thought of being mistaken for a young vegetable thief as she turned back to the soil.

She'd spent far too little time over the past few years growing things. Her parents' house in the Lake District had mainly lawns and flowerbeds, and she'd been living in a series of student rooms, or one-bedroom flats, where a few pot plants struggled to survive. It was time to stay in one place. Put down roots. Be more grounded.

There wasn't room for more than a few pots of herbs at the cottage, but maybe she could put her name down for a plot here. She'd always had her own patch of ground on her grandfather's allotment, where she'd grown a mixture of plants and battled with the weeds. She'd spent hours there.

Then she'd left for university and everything changed. Granddad and Grandma died within six months of each other, then her parents sold the family home and moved from Somerset to the Lake District.

They'd been planning the move for years, so it was no surprise, but when she first visited them in their new house she'd felt disorientated. Her parents were as loving as ever, but they'd made new circles of friends and were out and about enjoying their new life, while friends and acquaintances she'd grown up with were hundreds of miles away.

She'd slept in the guest room. Her own bedroom, with its posters, photographs and memories of sleepovers with friends, had gone. Her mother hadn't thrown anything away. Everything had been carefully packed into boxes for her to sort out. She never had. As far as she knew the boxes were still in the loft in the new house.

Her first nursing post after university had been in a city, where she was lonely, knew no-one and felt anonymous. Was that part of the reason she'd been so easily taken in by Justin? She'd wanted to believe his lies and promises. And he had been devastatingly handsome. Tall and fit. Dark, almost black hair, tanned skin, deep brown eyes with a sardonic glint. He'd made her laugh. When had she first realised his humour was cruel and spiteful, and almost always at someone else's expense? Not soon enough. How easy it was to be fooled by physical attraction. How was anyone to know if a ready smile hid a controlling manner, or a vicious temper?

An image of Meg's photograph of Mike's laughing face flashed into her mind. He wasn't good-looking in the conventional way. His appeal was in his open grin, his cheerful face, his friendliness.

Why hadn't she mentioned to Meg that she had met him? She'd been startled at the time, but there had been several occasions since, when Meg had been talking about her family, that she could have said something. Her neighbour was obviously very fond of all her relatives, but especially of Mike. He seemed as close to her as a grandson would be. He would surely come to visit when he found out about her accident.

Once again, the thought of seeing Mike set her pulse racing. It was a warning sign. If they met, she'd have to be friendly, for Meg's sake, but she'd avoid him if she could. She didn't need any complications in her life.

The sound of children playing broke into her thoughts. She hadn't meant to stay so long. Quickly, she took a few photographs to show Meg what she'd done, and console her that her plot was still looking cared for, then put the garden fork back in the shed, picked up the tin of seeds and basket of vegetables, and left.

It took her longer to reach the gate than it had done to walk up. Word had spread quickly, and it seemed everyone wanted to send Meg their best wishes.

The children she'd heard were with their mothers on a plot near the gate, and sent their love to 'Aunty Meg'.

She was humming cheerfully as she neared home. The few hours at the allotment had brought back so many happy memories. She'd offer to help for as long as it took Meg to be able to use her arm properly again.

10

Mike edged his car carefully into the space outside Meg's cottage. He'd left home before dawn and was ready for an early lunch; if she was well enough, he hoped to take her out for a meal.

He admired the tubs of geraniums as he rang the bell. Aunt Meg hadn't lost her touch where growing plants was concerned. There was no sign of movement inside the cottage, so he knocked at the door and called out.

'Aunt Meg? Are you there?'

He heard her coming towards the door and grinned as she opened it, expecting her usual cheery welcome. He was disappointed. Her initial delight was quickly replaced by a scowl of disapproval.

'What are you doing here? Mind my arm. I've broken it. But you'll know that, won't you? Your mother sent you to fetch me, didn't she?'

'She didn't send me, I offered to come,' Mike said. 'Are you going to let me in?'

As he followed her into the living room, she continued grumbling.

'I'm not coming. I told her not to send George. Did she think I'd listen to you? Your mother means well, but I'm not going back to Sheffield. I'm better off here. I'm being well looked after.'

She looked cross, but not unwell, and she certainly sounded as spirited as ever.

'Mum said someone was helping you.'

'My new neighbour, Amy. She's a lovely girl. You may meet her later. How long are you staying?'

'Trying to get rid of me already?' Mike teased.

'I was thinking about lunch,' she said.

'I thought I'd take you out, if your broken arm hasn't ruined your appetite. Then I need to drive over to Manchester. I've an interview first thing in the morning, so I've booked into a hotel overnight.'

Finally she beamed at him, and hugged him with her good arm, giving him the sort of welcome he was used to.

'That's wonderful news. I'm sorry, Mike. I was sure you'd come to try to persuade me to come back to Sheffield.'

He followed her into the kitchen. 'I was going to come and see you after the interview, but when Mum told me about your accident I thought I'd come today and put her mind at rest. I was concerned, too. You wouldn't like it if we didn't care.'

'That's true.' Meg grinned up at him. 'I'm a cantankerous old woman.'

Mike didn't disagree. He stood watching, but made no effort to help as she slowly set out the mugs and reached in the fridge for the milk.

'You're welcome to come back tomorrow and tell me how you got on,' she said. 'Might you be coming to live nearby?'

'If this interview goes well, I could be living near enough to come for tea. You could bake me cakes,' he said. 'You did that very well,' he added, as she passed him his tea. 'Sorry I didn't help. I wanted to see how well you managed.'

'I knew that was what you were doing. If you want a chocolate biscuit, you'll have to get one yourself. There's some there. I asked Amy to buy some yesterday; she doesn't eat enough.'

Mike reached for the jar, which had stood on the highest kitchen shelf since he and Lynda were children. It used to contain sweets, and now it was half-full of small chocolate bars. He took one, and offered one to Aunt Meg, but she opted for a plain tea biscuit from the accessible tin by the kettle.

'Don't be cross, Aunt Meg. I need to be able to tell Mum you're being sensible, then she won't stress so much. She's enough to worry about with Grannie being so difficult.'

Meg sighed. 'Lily's more than enough for her to cope with. That's why I keep telling your mother not to take on so much. She's no need to fret about me.'

'Which is what I'll tell her,' Mike said. 'Now, come on. I want to know all about your accident. How did you come to fall?'

'It was so silly. A moment's careless-ness. I was coming out of the leisure centre, thinking about breakfast, my mind on what I had to do up at...'

'Hang on a minute, Aunt Meg. You were coming out of the leisure centre, thinking about breakfast? What on earth were you doing at the leisure centre? And what time was it for goodness' sake?'

'Swimming. I always go early. What did you think I was doing? Circuits?'

'You still go swimming? I remember we used to go when Mum brought us over to stay, when we were children.'

'I go every week. More often if the weather's bad and I can't get out with the walking group.'

'Walking group!' Mike wasn't sure whether to laugh or scold.

'No need to look so disapproving. I don't go rambling across the mountains on my own any more.'

'I knew you went for walks with your friends, but ... '

'There's about eight of us. We don't do the higher ridges, but I bet I could still keep up with you. There's no need to tell your mother.'

'I'll tell her about the swimming. She'll approve of that. She goes herself every Sunday morning, early, like you do. She says she swims all the tension away.'

They sat quietly for a while. Mike was thinking about his mother, and the hard time she was having looking after her own mother. He'd be able to reassure her when he went home.

'Mum thought once you'd moved here, and got rid of the house and its huge garden, you'd start to act your age. You're not going to, though, are you?' he said.

'I admit I've slowed up a bit, but the swimming and walking keep me fit.'

'Until now.' Mike frowned, nodding at her arm.

'I remember you breaking your leg when you were playing rugby at school,' Meg retorted. 'no-one suggested then you give up all activities. This is the first time in my life I've broken a bone. It's not as if I'm doing it all the time.'

81

'Hey, Aunt Meg. Don't be so touchy. You'll have to be careful. Bones heal quicker when you're young. You may find you need a walking stick for a while, to help with your balance.'

'I wish you'd stop talking to me as if I'm stupid,' Meg snapped. 'I use walking poles when I go out with the group. If I need to use them around the village, I will.'

'Sorry,' Mike said. His aunt was very edgy. It wasn't like her. He didn't think she was as well as she was pretending to be. He tried to think of something non-controversial to talk about.

'I was admiring your geraniums as I waited for you to come to the door,' he said. 'They're beautiful. Not too much to cope with. It must be such a relief, not having to worry about the garden. If you were still in the old house you'd have been almost demented by now, fretting about the vegetables, the lawn and the hedge cutting. You'd have pushed me out the door with a garden fork in my hand before I'd taken my coat off.'

'Are you saying I pestered you to do things for me? I didn't mean to. I'm trying to manage on my own. Amy says she's happy to help, but how can she be, young girl like her? Do I take advantage of people, Mike?'

He saw that her hand was shaking as she placed her empty cup back on the coffee table, and hurried to reassure her.

'Aunt Meg, it's almost impossible to do anything for you, you're so independent. I was teasing you. I don't mind doing anything for you, when you let me.'

She sat back in her chair, nursing her arm, her face shuttered, her eyes almost closed. She must be in more pain than she was admitting.

'Is your arm hurting?' he asked. 'Would you prefer not to go out for lunch? I'll go and buy something and make sandwiches.'

'For goodness' sake, Mike! Stop fussing. I'm perfectly well enough to go out. I was thinking about my garden.'

'We had some good times working on it, didn't we? I learnt a lot. I'd like a big garden when I eventually buy a house.'

'I did miss my garden,' she said, hesitantly. 'I missed it a lot. I...'

'You must have. It was a big part of your life. But Mum was right. It was too much for you, and it was too far for us to keep coming to help.'

'I thought you came because you liked coming, not because I needed you to mow my lawns.'

Her voice was rising as she spoke. She was almost shouting.

Mike was becoming seriously concerned. He loved coming to visit. He'd do anything for her, but because he wanted to, not because anyone asked him. He'd never known her so agitated.

'Aunt Meg, you need to calm down,' he said.

'I don't need to do anything. I wish you'd all stop nagging me. Don't do this, don't do that, be careful. I am careful. I don't have to ask anyone's permission to do things.'

She was really upset. Was it shock after her fall or had she been fretting about things for a while? She obviously didn't think she could tell his mother half of what she was doing. And why shouldn't she continue to do the things she enjoyed, as long as she was able to? Did she think he would try to restrict her, too? Was she frightened her broken arm wouldn't heal?

He didn't know what to do. She'd slumped back in her chair after her outburst and sat staring at the vase of flowers on the hearth, her face crumpled with misery.

He went across to her, intending to give her a gentle hug, but as he bent towards her she pushed him away.

'Leave me alone!' she shouted, sounding uncannily like his young nephew when he was having a strop.

Hoping to make her laugh, he responded in kind.

'Right then, I will!' he yelled.

He saw amusement replace anger in her eyes, and sighed with relief as he crouched on the floor beside her.

'If you can't treat Mrs Evans with

respect, I think you should leave.'

They both turned to see who had come into the room, and Mike leapt to his feet as he saw the girl from the aqueduct standing in the doorway, clutching a basketful of vegetables. Surprise and delight were swiftly followed by dismay as she glared at him, her hazel eyes furious.

11

Amy let herself into Meg's cottage, intending to have a quick chat with her about the allotment, and leave the vegetables in the kitchen, before going home to rest. This first night back on duty was always difficult. It was impossible to sleep much, yet she needed to be alert for the twelve-hour shift. Tomorrow would be different. She'd have breakfast with Meg, then go home to sleep. Her neighbour was insisting she'd be able to cope on her own during the day, but had promised to reconsider going to stay with Gwen if necessary.

Before she could call out a greeting, she heard Meg shouting.

'Leave me alone!'

Amy didn't hesitate as she heard a man's voice shouting back.

'Right then, I will!'

She pushed open the door, and years

of training and experience took over as she leapt to defend her patient.

'If you can't treat Mrs Evans with respect, I think you should leave.'

Her anger evaporated, leaving her confused, as Meg chuckled. Her visitor leapt to his feet and turned towards her, his face a confused mixture of dismay and recognition.

Mike! The man she'd been unable to stop thinking about for the past few weeks. He didn't seem at all pleased to see her. Small wonder. She'd just caught him shouting at his aunt.

Not that Meg seemed distressed.

'Amy, this is my great-nephew, Mike,' she said. 'Mike, this is my neighbour, Amy. She's been helping me.'

'We've met before,' Amy said, coolly.

'I remember,' Mike said. 'Great to meet you again, Amy. Sorry you over-heard us arguing.'

She stood glaring at him. He looked less like a bully than a little boy caught out in a misdemeanour.

'This is not like it seems,' he stuttered.

Meg was certainly showing no signs of being cowed by him, even if he did tower over her. She appeared more amused than frightened. Amy waited for an explanation.

'Aunt Meg and I were sort of ... '

'Sparring,' Meg said, firmly. 'What my great-nephew is trying to say is that he was attempting to organise my life and I was resisting. You're quite right, Amy,' she added. 'He should treat me with more respect.'

'But Aunt Meg...'

His aunt interrupted again. 'Mike was trying to tell me what to do. We ended up arguing, as we used to when he was a child, as much play-acting as anything. We were quite enjoying ourselves.'

'Speak for yourself, Aunt Meg. You were winning.'

'Because I was right.'

Amy watched the banter between them and relaxed a little. They were obviously very fond of each other.

'But I don't tell you what to do,' Mike protested. 'I'd already agreed not to tell

Mum about the mountain walking.'

'Mountain walking!' Amy interrupted.

'Would you believe it, Amy? My aunt goes out walking on the mountains every week. She's upset because she won't be able to go for a while.'

'I remember you telling me you went out walking with a group of friends the day I moved in,' Amy said. 'I thought you'd be walking along the canal or the river. You never told me you still went up into the mountains, Meg.'

'I suppose you think I should sit in a chair for the rest of my life as well,' Meg grumbled.

'Not at all. Can I come with you when your arm is better? I'd love to have company while I explore the area.'

'You'd be welcome,' Meg said. 'There's a few of us go, but we're all elderly. You'd soon get bored and want to tackle longer routes. You see, Mike? Amy doesn't want me to stop doing things.'

'I don't either,' Mike said. He turned to Amy.

'It's my mother who gets stressed with

Aunt Meg being so far away. She'll be happy that Aunt Meg still goes swimming, but I agreed not to tell her about the walking group. She'd be worrying and there's no need.'

'She's got enough to worry about.' Meg nodded. 'But then you started saying it was a good thing I don't have to worry about struggling with gardening anymore ... '

'And you lost your temper. What was that about?'

Amy was suddenly aware she was clutching a basket of freshly harvested produce from an allotment he obviously knew nothing about, while behind him Meg was frantically signalling for her not to tell him.

'Nothing really,' Meg said. 'I seem to be a bit short-tempered at the moment. Blame it on my broken arm. Weren't you going to treat me to lunch out?'

'Why don't you join us, Amy?' Mike suggested.

Amy saw Meg's sudden flare of interest as she looked from one to the other.

For a moment she was tempted to accept, but she was too confused about her feelings towards Mike to feel comfortable in his company, and Meg wouldn't want her anywhere near her precious great-nephew if she knew about Justin.

'Did you say you'd met Mike before?' Meg asked, as the silence grew uncomfortable. 'You never mentioned it when I showed you his photograph.'

'We had a brief conversation a few weeks ago, when we both happened to be walking across the aqueduct at the same time. When I saw your photograph I thought Mike looked like the man I'd met, but wasn't sure. It seemed too much of a coincidence. We hadn't exchanged names.'

She was ashamed at the ease with which the lie slipped out. She hadn't wanted to deceive Meg.

'So, now you have been introduced, will you come for lunch with us?' Meg asked.

'I can't,' Amy said. 'I need to rest before working tonight.'

'That's what you said last time we met,' Mike sighed.

Neither tried to persuade her. If they had she would have refused, yet she was perversely disappointed as she left, still clutching the basket of vegetables.

12

Mike had been about to follow Amy from the room when his aunt stopped him. 'Amy needs her rest,' she'd insisted.

'But I need to explain to her. To make sure she understands I wasn't shouting at you, not really.'

'She'll call in to see me before she goes to work. I'll make sure she knows we were only bickering.'

'I hope she does. It must have looked terrible from her point of view.'

'And her opinion matters to you? I thought you'd only met her once.' Mike felt his face redden as she looked at him searchingly.

'I have. It's just that I wouldn't like her to think badly of me.' He shuffled uncomfortably as she continued to stare at him. 'Are we going out for lunch or not?'

'How's Emma?' she asked as he helped

her on with her coat.

'I've no idea,' Mike said. 'I told you we'd split up. She's probably lounging on Eduardo's yacht somewhere exotic.'

He didn't add that any lingering thoughts he might have had about his ex had been driven from his mind the moment he met Amy.

Over lunch they'd chatted about the many holidays he and his sister had spent in the area as children, about Lynda's young son, about his hopes for the interview tomorrow. He was relieved to see her relax as they ate, though she looked tired and didn't object when he took her home.

Then it was time to go, but before he left he promised to come back next day, to tell her how the interview had gone.

He drove across to Manchester, his mind whirling with the events of the day. It seemed ages, not a few hours, since he'd been standing by the project site. Once he booked in at the hotel he needed to concentrate on preparing for the interview tomorrow. He really wanted this job. Not just because it was the type of work he wanted to do, in an area he loved. It would mean he could live near enough to Aunt Meg to call to see her frequently.

And now he'd found the girl from the aqueduct. He'd hardly been able to believe it when he'd seen her standing in his aunt's living room. Then he'd seen the fury on her face, her hazel eyes glaring at him. Her voice had been withering as she told him to treat Mrs Evans with respect.

She obviously thought he'd been shouting at his aunt. She was right. He had been shouting. But he'd been teasing, not angry. And Aunt Meg had been yelling back. Playing along. She'd been amused. It had been the first spark of the spirited Aunt Meg he knew, that he'd seen since he'd arrived.

Aunt Meg had defended him, laughing, telling Amy they'd only been sparring with each other, but he winced as he realised how it must have sounded to an onlooker. If only there had been time to explain.

Once he booked in at the hotel, he phoned his mother and reassured her that Meg was recovering. He didn't mention his concerns. There was nothing his mother could do, unless he took his aunt to Sheffield, and Mike instinctively knew that would slow her recovery rather than helping it.

'What about the neighbour?' his mother asked.

Mike was on firmer ground here. There was no doubt Amy was competent, willing to help and seemed genuinely fond of Aunt Meg. There was no need to add that she had invaded his thoughts so completely he was hardly able to think, or that her laugh was infectious, her disapproval devastating.

'Amy is being very kind, looking after Aunt Meg. She's going to continue to go in morning and evening,' he said.

'That's a lot to expect from a new neighbour.'

'I think she's glad to be able to help. I'm going to go back tomorrow before I come home, but I don't think you need to worry, Mum.'

'That's a relief,' Gwen said, before launching into a rambling tale about what his young nephew had said when Lynda had brought him to visit that afternoon.

He was only half-listening. He was thinking about Amy, wondering if he would be able to talk to her the following evening, before he left for Sheffield.

'Lynda says her mother's really worried. It's not like Emma, is it?'

Mention of his ex jolted his concentration back to the current conversation.

'What's not like Emma?'

'I've just been telling you, Mike. Weren't you listening? Lynda says she bumped into Emma's mother in the supermarket. She's worried because she hasn't heard from her for weeks.'

'She's probably having too good a time to keep writing home,' Mike said.

'Her mother told Lynda she had a postcard from Lisbon, then one from a village in the Alentejo, then another from the Azores, but that was weeks ago. She's heard nothing since.'

'She's lucky to have had postcards. It was more usual for Emma to send short emails. Hasn't she phoned?'

'Apparently not. Lynda said Emma always contacted her mother when she went abroad, sending messages and posting pictures on Facebook.'

'That's true. She always kept in touch.'

'Lynda says it's not like her.'

'It wasn't like her to go off with someone she'd only just met,' Mike said impatiently. 'What's this got to do with me?'

'I thought you'd be interested, that's all. You haven't heard from her, have you? If you have, you should phone her parents. Let them know she's safe.'

Mike sighed. Unlike Aunt Meg, his mother hadn't been relieved when Emma had left him. She was certain Mike was hiding his distress, and was secretly hoping for a reconciliation. Nothing he said seemed to convince her otherwise.

'I haven't heard from Emma since she

went off with Eduardo. If her parents are worried, they should phone her,' he said.

'Apparently her mobile's gone dead.'

'She's travelling, Mum. She's probably out of range of a signal. I have to go. I'll speak to you when I get home.'

All thoughts of Emma faded as he turned his attention to preparing for his interview. It was harder to keep Amy out of his mind. Now he'd found she was living at Hen Bont, he had an added incentive to try to convince the interview panel they should give him the job.

13

When Amy returned to her own cottage she dumped the vegetables in her kitchen, ate a cheese sandwich, then took a book upstairs with her, hoping a quiet read would lull her to sleep.

It was hard to concentrate on the story. She heard Meg and Mike go out to his car. Meg was laughing at something he was saying. They were obviously very fond of each other.

For a moment she'd been tempted to accept his offer for her to join them for lunch. It was kind of him to ask her after the way she'd spoken to him. How could she have thought he was threatening his aunt?

When she'd heard Mike's raised voice, all her bitterness towards Justin had flooded back. She had wanted to lash out, to say all the things she'd been too upset and frightened to say to him at the time.

But Mike wasn't her ex. Justin would have been furious if she'd dared to criticise him, but when she'd burst in, ordering Mike to leave his aunt alone, he hadn't been at all cross. He had been very embarrassed, though.

Unexpectedly she giggled as she remembered his stumbling attempts to explain. It was as if he was expecting to be sent to the naughty step. He would have been an adorable child. With those huge blue eyes and that innocent look, it would have been difficult to chastise him. It was even harder to resist him now. The warmth of his voice set her senses spinning.

He wasn't at all like Justin, but he might well be in a relationship. She remembered the girl in the photograph on Meg's sideboard, and Meg's dismissive comment that she was a friend of Mike's.

Yet another reason to resist the attraction she felt towards him. But she was ashamed of the way she'd behaved. She probably owed him an apology.

His concern for Meg was justified. She'd been anxious herself about how her neighbour would cope with being confined indoors over the next few weeks. Only this morning she'd discouraged her from going to the allotment, and it would have done her good. What she needed was a bit of help and encouragement, not constant lists of things she should no longer do.

As long as she always kept a mobile phone with her, why shouldn't she keep doing the things she enjoyed? She certainly wasn't short of friends.

Remembering her morning at the allotment, and how many people had asked how Meg was, she drifted off into a fitful sleep, planning to take her to visit as soon as she could.

She heard Mike's car return, turned over and dozed again. When she woke next it was to hear Meg calling, 'Goodbye, and good luck!' as he drove off.

Good luck? What was that about? None of her business. It was time to get ready for work, but she went to see Meg first.

'Mike's gone off to Manchester,' Meg said. 'Would you like a drink and a slice of this cake his mother sent with him? It'll be delicious. Gwen's like her mother in that. Poor Lily. She was such a good cook. Now she wouldn't recognise half the ingredients.'

'Did you enjoy your lunch?' Amy asked. 'I can't stay long but I can have a quick cup of tea with you. I came to check you were all right before I go to work. I thought you wouldn't want another meal tonight.'

'A piece of cake is all I can manage,' Meg said. 'We had a lovely lunch. I should have persuaded you to come with us, but I was horrified when I saw you standing there with the basket of vegetables.'

'But why? You asked me to go and fetch them.'

'I'd been having a disagreement with Mike,' Meg said.

'I know. I heard.'

'I didn't want him to find out I'd rented

an allotment. He'd already agreed not to tell his mother about the mountain walking.'

'I must admit I was surprised to hear about that.'

'Not you as well,' Meg sighed. 'I go with a group of friends. We've been walking together for years. We're careful and responsible, but I'm not stopping just because other people can't deal with it. It's like being a teenager again, having to fight for every scrap of independence.'

'Meg, I'm not trying to stop you doing anything. I think it's great that you go walking. I meant it when I asked if I could go with you. I'd like to get up into the mountains myself.'

'You need to be going with young people, not spending all your spare time with an old lady.'

'We'll talk about it when you're ready to start walking again,' Amy said. 'But I still don't understand why you didn't want to tell Mike about your allotment.'

'I was so lucky to get that plot within walking distance. I should have mentioned it ages ago, when I first got the tenancy. But I've made my own choices since before Gwen was born. I'd only been married a few years when my husband died. We had wanted a family, but not straight away. We thought we had plenty of time.'

'I'm sorry,' Amy said.

'It's all a long time ago, but I've had to make my own life. I'm not used to having to defend my decisions.'

'But why would Mike object to you having an allotment?'

'I'm not sure he would, not really, but I didn't want to start arguing with him again. I'd been irritable from the moment he arrived. I've been like it all week. One minute I think I'm doing well, the next I can't do the simplest thing. It's so frustrating, but that's no excuse for shouting at Mike. He was only being concerned.'

'But you've always been cheerful when I've been with you. I didn't realise how low you were feeling.'

'I'm so grateful to you, Amy. I didn't want you to see me stroppy.'

'And you didn't mind if Mike did?'

'He knows what I can be like, and he did provoke me. He was saying what a good thing it was I didn't still have the garden. How fortunate it was that he didn't need to be mowing my lawns or cutting my hedges. I felt so guilty. I'd been thinking I was managing on my own. But I haven't, have I? I've been relying on you.'

'I've only been cooking you a few meals.'

'I'd just sent you to check my allotment. If I had still had my garden, Mike would have been outside raking up the leaves for me, pretending he was enjoying himself.'

'So you got cross?'

'At myself, really. But Mike was there, and I took it out on him. I shouted at him. He shouted back. I was cross, but he was trying to make me laugh. Then you walked in.'

'Carrying a basket full of vegetables.'

Amy laughed and Meg joined in.

'It was a bit childish, wasn't it? I will

tell him about my gardening, but all in good time. It seemed like too much information when he'd just learnt about the swimming and the walking.'

'So the allotment is our secret, at the moment.' Amy grinned. 'I won't say anything.'

'I'm not sure whether to write to the council and give the lease up. It'll be ages before I can do any work, and the weeds will be taking over. Better to let someone younger have the space.'

'It's almost the end of the season. You'll feel differently in the spring and wish you'd kept it on.'

'Was it looking too bad?' Meg asked.

'Not at all. It was much tidier than most plots. I took some photos.'

Amy reached for her mobile and showed Meg the pictures she'd taken.

'I brought the tin of seeds from the shed,' she said. 'And did a little weeding as I dug up the vegetables. I was wondering if you'd like me to drive you up there on my next day off. I noticed a chair in the shed. You could sit outside and tell

108

me what you want doing.'

Meg didn't reply. She sat looking at the photographs, tears rolling down her face.

'I'm sorry. I didn't mean to upset you,' Amy said. 'I thought you might like to go, but I can see it would be horrible watching someone else, when you wanted to do the work yourself.'

'It's not that,' Meg said. 'It's just that you're so kind. Spending all your time with a grumpy old lady. You must have much more exciting things to do.'

Amy thought of her empty cottage, her non-existent circle of friends, and her far-away family. 'To be honest, no, I don't. I'd love to help. I could tidy up ready for the winter. When is the lease due to be renewed?'

'Next March,' Meg said.

'There you are, then. Don't decide yet. Tell your nephew about it when you're ready to. I won't say anything. I'm hardly likely to see him, am I?'

'You may well do,' Meg said. 'He's going for a job interview tomorrow, and he's coming here afterwards to tell me about it. If he gets the work, he won't be living far away. If he has time to take me out for a meal again, would you like to join us? I think you'd both get on well.'

Amy hesitated. A meal with Mike, time to talk to him, a chance to apologise? Then common sense took over. She found his presence far too disturbing for comfort. Best to keep her distance.

'No thanks, Meg. I don't think so. I'll be sleeping most of the day and you won't want me tagging along. What sort of work does Mike do?'

'Usually he's all over the world working on big engineering projects. But this is something to do with canal renovation. He said it was to construct a flyover for a bypass, and rebuild a flight of locks. The canal has been derelict for years.'

'Sounds very muddy,' Amy said, imagining Mike wielding a shovel, his wellington boots deep in stagnant canal water.

'It does, rather.' Meg smiled. 'He was always one to be getting in the mud as a child, never happier than when he was splodging about in puddles. And on the beach, when Lynda vvas building sandcastles, he was busy constructing miniature waterways down to the sea to link up with the moat. They came to stay with me often. We used to tramp all over the mountains. They were happy days.'

Amy said goodbye and went back to her cottage for a shower before leaving for work. Meg certainly seemed happy that Mike might be coming to be living nearby. Maybe he'd find time to take his aunt for a few country walks when he wasn't up to his ankles in canal mud.

He'd be good company. It was easy to imagine herself striding along the mountain tracks with him. Not that he would suggest it. Not that she would accept if he did.

14

When Mike walked out of the company offices next day he thought the interview had gone well. He'd been impressed with the organisation, and was sure he wanted this work, but he'd been told there were other candidates, and that he wouldn't hear anything for a few weeks. All he could do was wait.

He drove back to Hen Bont, anxious to see how Aunt Meg was before he headed back to Sheffield, but he needn't have worried. She was cheerful and welcoming, with no sign of the snappish behaviour of the previous day.

'Will you stay overnight?' she asked, as she made him tea.

'Sorry, I'll have to go by early evening. I have to be back at work tomorrow. But I do want to speak to Amy before she goes to work.'

'She'll be awake soon. She said she'd

come to see me before she leaves for work but she may change her mind when she sees your car.'

'Because she's avoiding me?' Mike said.

'Because she knows I'm not on my own. Why should she avoid you?'

'She thinks I was bullying you yesterday,' Mike said.

'No, she doesn't. I explained what happened. Drink your tea and tell me about your interview.'

'The interview went well,' Mike said. 'But I won't know for a while if I've got the work. And I phoned Mum and said you were coping well. She's got something else to worry about now. Emma's not been in contact with her parents.'

'Emma! Why's Gwen worried about her? I thought you said she'd gone off sailing with a Portuguese man she met in Lisbon.'

'She has. But her mother told Lynda she hasn't heard from her for while.'

Mike told his aunt the story, intending it to be a light-hearted distraction for her, but as he repeated the details, or lack of them, he realised how unusual it was for the girl he'd known for so many years not to keep in touch with her parents.

'She's probably too busy having a good time to keep contacting home,' Aunt Meg said.

'That's what I said. Going off like that in the first place was out of character, so why should anyone be surprised when she doesn't keep phoning? Mum seemed to think I might have heard from her.'

'You haven't, have you?'

'No. And I don't expect to. We parted on good terms. But it was very final. It is odd, though.'

'Don't you start worrying,' Aunt Meg said. 'Leave that to your mother. She's the expert.'

★ ★ ★

Amy heard a car being parked in the courtyard and assumed it was Mike arriving back from Manchester. She had been about to call on Meg to see if she needed anything, but started getting ready for work instead.

It was better to avoid Mike. She was managing to ignore thoughts of him while she was awake, but she'd not long woken from a complicated dream in which he had featured, rescuing her from a series of bizarre situations. She didn't need rescuing. She was managing perfectly well. She was starting a new life in a lovely village. She had a responsible job, which she enjoyed.

She felt irrationally irritated with him. How dare he invade her dreams! She hoped he'd parked carefully. She was used to having the parking space to herself. There was only just room for two cars and she didn't want to have to knock and ask him to move his. She peered through the window to check and saw him standing in the pouring rain, his hand raised, about to knock on her door.

It was too late to retreat and pretend she was out. He'd seen her and waved. Reluctantly, she opened the door. She could hardly leave him standing there. Not only was he getting soaking wet, the rain was beating in.

'Come in,' she said, grudgingly. 'I can't stop, though. I need to leave for work soon.'

'I know,' he said quickly. 'Aunt Meg told me. But I have to drive back to Sheffield tonight, and I didn't want to go before apologising for yesterday. We got off to a bad start, I think.'

'You apologised yesterday. And it was your aunt you were shouting at, not me. It's her you should be apologising to.'

'I have. But, to be fair, she had been shouting at me before you arrived. She said she'd told you what happened.'

'She did explain,' Amy said. 'I overreacted. I'm sorry, but for a moment I thought you were … '

' … bullying my Aunt Meg,' Mike said, ruefully. 'It must have sounded awful when you came in. But I'd never do anything to upset her. Really, I wouldn't. She's a very special lady.'

Mike stood looking earnestly at her, a

worried frown creasing his brow. His hair was flopping over his face and a trickle of rainwater was dripping off it and running down his cheek.

She felt an overwhelming desire to wipe his hair dry, but contented herself with handing him a towel.

'You do understand, don't you?' he asked, as he rubbed his hair and face dry. 'She'd got so upset, and I was only trying to make her see sense and take more care. I don't want her falling over again.'

'I understand, but you don't want her losing confidence either,' Amy said. 'Constant nagging isn't going to help her get back to her normal routine.'

'But should she get back to normal? She still thinks she's able to do the things she's always done, and she can't. Surely it's time she accepted that.'

'Maybe she does need to be more cautious,' Amy said. 'But if she gives up all her activities, she'll never get her strength back. She'll be having the strapping off soon and then she'll need to be encouraged to use that arm, not wrapped up in a shawl and told she's too old to do anything.'

'But should she keep on with things like walking up mountains?'

'Why not? If she's always with others and they choose the route sensibly?'

'I only want what's best for her. She's very important to me, my Aunt Meg. She's a very sparky lady.'

'She certainly is.' Amy smiled. That was something they could both agree on.

'Friends?' he asked.

'Friends,' she agreed. 'Now, I have to get ready for work, so I'm afraid … '

'Yes, I'll go. I'll be over again at the weekend, to see how Aunt Meg's getting on. Maybe we could go out for a drink?'

Amy hesitated. She needed to be civil with Mike, especially if he was going to be calling on his aunt frequently, but she wanted to keep her distance as well.

'I'm not sure when I'll be working,' she began, but Mike already seemed to have thought better of his suggestion.

'On second thoughts, why don't I take you and Aunt Meg out for a meal? We can arrange whether it's lunch or dinner when I arrive. You've been doing so much for her, it's the least I can do, and I know she'd enjoy it.'

Amy could hardly say no. Meg would certainly be pleased, and going for a meal with them both would be innocent enough.

She closed the door and got ready for work, trying not to think about those blue eyes, the way he smiled, the way his hair looked when it was tousled by the towel. It was so simple to decide not to be attracted by someone, so difficult when that person was standing beside her, looking down at her, setting all her nerves jangling with anticipation.

15

Meg stood on her doorstep for a while after waving goodbye to Mike. The rain had passed over at last and stars were beginning to appear. Amy had already left for work. Her cottage was in darkness, and the courtyard was silent. The ginger cat stalked across the cobbles and past Meg's feet, ignoring her completely, before jumping up onto the wall and crouching there, staring intently into the dark shrubbery below.

She watched as the animal grew tense, quivered, then leapt down into the overgrown garden and disappeared. She envied the cat its freedom to roam. She felt unsettled. If it had been summer, she would have gone for an evening stroll, but setting off on the wet pavements, in the dark, with a broken arm, was probably not a good idea.

Reluctantly, she went back indoors

and switched on the television, but soon lost interest in the complicated lives of the characters onscreen. She made herself a drink and sat, half-listening to the radio, while her mind wandered. Mike had promised to phone as soon as he reached home. She hoped he would get the job at Betteley Locks. He seemed really keen. He'd probably rent somewhere to live near the site, but it would be good to have him nearby, calling in when he had time to spare.

Gwen would worry less if Mike was living near enough to visit, though she would soon find something else to fret about, bless her, like this concern over Emma. It was unlike the girl to lose contact with her family. Meg didn't think she'd caused her parents a moment's worry, even during her teenage years. It would have been such a shock when she threw away her career, and her relationship with Mike, to sail off with a stranger. But she was used to travelling with her work. She could fly home if things didn't work out with the romance.

Meg could see why Emma's parents were perturbed, but it was certainly no concern of Mike's. Emma had left him. He needed to be making new friends, not thinking about why his former girlfriend wasn't contacting her parents.

He'd known Emma so long that it would be hard for him to get out of the habit of looking out for her. Was that all it was? Or did he miss the girl more than he admitted?

She had been so sure he was attracted to Amy, and though Amy had disguised it well, Meg thought the interest was mutual. She had been strongly tempted to try some subtle matchmaking, but Amy had never talked about her personal life. Was there an absentee boyfriend or a broken romance? There was a deep sadness in her eyes, when she was unguarded. She was a lovely girl and Meg didn't want her hurt.

★ ★ ★

The following morning she had breakfast with Amy, as usual. The girl was tired, but cheerful, and entertained Meg with a humorous story Sally had told her. Meg told her Mike had phoned when he reached home, watching closely for her reaction, but Amy simply nodded, before going home to sleep.

Meg wandered restlessly around her tiny cottage. She was thinking more rationally this morning, and could see that Mike's concern about Emma had been that of a friend, not that of a rejected lover. She knew he wouldn't deliberately hurt Amy, or anyone else. It wasn't in his nature to be thoughtless or unkind.

She needed to get out. If she stayed inside much longer she'd be trying to run everyone's lives for them. She decided to walk to the corner shop to buy a magazine. It was a sunny morning, but cold, and there was no way she could put her coat on over her sling. She pulled a thick cloak out from the back of the cupboard.

'Fortunate you hadn't thrown this out, Meg,' she muttered. 'Not the height of fashion, but it'll keep you warm over the next few weeks. Better take your walking pole for balance. Don't want to slip and cause people even more trouble. And stop talking to yourself, it'll get to be a habit.'

As she opened the door she saw Madge and Emrys coming into the courtyard.

'Where do you think you're going?' Madge called.

'Just to buy a magazine.'

'I'll go and get it for you,' Emrys offered.

'I need the fresh air. There's nothing wrong with my legs. I need to be careful not to slip, that's all.'

'Why don't we walk around the corner to Pete's café?' Madge said. 'We could treat ourselves to hot chocolate. Then we can go to the newsagent's.

There may be a few other things you need, and Emrys can carry them back for you.'

'I don't really need anything. The magazine was an excuse to go out. I've started talking to myself. Not a good sign.'

'Madge talks to herself all the time,'

Emrys said.

'That's because I'm the only one who listens. And I give myself good advice,' Madge said.

Meg chuckled. 'Pete's café it is, then. I feel better already. We can have a good gossip and put the world to rights.'

Meg was unsteady at first, but gained confidence with every step as she walked along between Madge and Emrys. By the time she returned home she was feeling much more positive about things. She'd be able to go for a short walk each day, as long as she took her walking pole.

Amy had a day off on Friday and promised to drive her to the allotment. It was going to be a good weekend. Mike phoned to say he'd be coming Saturday morning. Normally she'd have been preparing his bed, baking a cake and planning to look after him, but he'd made her promise not to do anything.

'I'll make the bed when I arrive,' he said. 'Do you know when Amy is working this weekend?'

'I think she's off until Sunday,' Meg said.

'That's good. She promised to join us for a meal out.'

Meg could hear the smile in his voice. She hadn't been wrong. He was obviously attracted to her neighbour.

16

Amy turned off the High Street and drove slowly along the narrow, over-grown lane to the main entrance of the allotment site. There was a small area for parking, and she carefully manoeuvred her car into the only space left.

It was a beautiful clear day, chilly enough to need a warm coat, but dry and sunny, and it looked as if everyone who could was busy taking advantage of the respite in the weather.

'It seems strange to be driven here,' Meg said, as Amy opened the door and steadied her as she stepped out. 'I feel as if I haven't been for ages, and it's not much more than a week.'

They began to walk slowly along the path. Meg had brought her walking pole, and needed it for balance on the uneven ground. Amy wondered if it had been a good idea. The last thing Meg needed was another fall. Maybe they should have waited another week.

Meg paused, looking around her, taking deep breaths of the crisp air. She turned to Amy and beamed, obviously delighted to be back, and Amy's doubts faded.

It was little Henry who saw them first.

'Mum! It's Auntie Meg,' he called.

Alicia dropped her rake and came hurrying across, wiping her hands on her dungarees, before giving Meg a gentle hug.

'Oh, I'm so glad to see you,' she said. 'Amy told us what happened. Is your arm very painful?'

'Not too bad. On your own this morning?'

'I'm helping,' Henry said, waving his miniature trowel.

Meg laughed as he tottered off.

'The others will be along later,' Alicia said. 'Meg, if you want anything, you will ask, won't you? We'll all help.'

Almost every plot they passed had

someone working on it. They all stopped what they were doing and came across to chat. Amy stif Ied a giggle. Their progress along the path had become like a royal procession. Everyone wanted to ask Meg how she was feeling, and offer help.

Wilfred and Rita, who tended the plot three down from Meg's, offered tea and biscuits whenever they were ready for a break.

'Thanks, but I've brought a flask and sandwiches,' Amy said.

'It's not me who'll be needing the break, it's Amy,' Meg said. 'I'm not going to be doing anything. I'm going to sit in the chair and watch.'

'That'll be a first,' Rita said. 'You'll be trying to work one-handed within half an hour.'

'No chance. I won't bring her again if she doesn't behave,' Amy laughed. 'Meg will have to content herself with telling me what to do,'

By the time they reached her plot, Amy could see Meg was exhausted and ready to settle into the garden chair.

'I didn't realise I'd met so many people here,' she said, as she allowed Amy to tuck a warm blanket round her legs. 'I usually come in quietly by the small gate from the river path, and work on my own up here. I often don't speak to anyone all day. Unless Fred is working next door on his patch, and he doesn't say much.'

'You've no idea how much they all think of you,' Amy said, as she began working her way along the rows of late peas with the hoe. 'Alicia told me she hadn't got a clue about growing things, but that you were always ready to help them.'

She finished the hoeing and turned to ask what wanted doing next, only to see Meg was out of the chair and picking her way over the ground towards her. She was about to tell her to be careful, but restrained herself when she saw how sensible Meg was being, using her pole and walking slowly.

'Those peas and beans are nearly finished,' Meg said. 'They'll need stripping out soon and putting on the compost heap.'

'Why don't you list the things you want me to do over the next few weeks? We'll come when we can, and you can supervise.'

'It's too much to ask,' Meg said.

'You're not asking me. I'm asking you if you'll let me come and do some gardening on your allotment. I love it here. It would be so peaceful after a difficult shift at work. Just the thing to unwind.'

'I think I'll have to tell Mike about my allotment.' Meg said, when Amy stopped working and poured out the mugs of tea. 'I don't like having secrets from him, and if he does get this job he's applied for, he'll be coming frequently. He'll be bound to find out then.'

'I agree you should tell him. I doubt he'll try to stop you when he knows how much you love coming here. It's such a wonderful site and you know so many people. I think you've got the best plot. You can look down over the others.'

'Sometimes I spend a whole day up

here. I only pull out a few weeds and then sit watching the people walk along the footpath, or the canoeists on the river. Or I watch Bill down there, non-stop manicuring his soil. He's trying to grow the biggest vegetables on the site.'

Amy laughed, and turned to look at Bill. He had finished digging and was methodically cleaning his tools before locking them in his shed. He saw her watching, nodded, hesitated, and then began striding up the path towards them.

Amy walked to meet him.

'I'm not sure if I should mention this to Meg, or not,' he said quietly. 'But there's talk about this land being sold off for development. They say we'll all have to leave within the year.'

'That's really upsetting,' Amy said. 'But I think she'd want to know, if there's any truth in it.'

'What are you two ,whispering about?' Meg called.

'We're not whispering, we're chatting,' Amy said, as they both walked across to Meg. 'Last time I came, Bill accused me of stealing your vegetables.'

'You didn't tell me that, Amy.'

'I forgot,' Amy said. 'I got a bit distracted when I got home.'

She blushed, remembering just how distracted she had been by Mike's presence in Meg's cottage. Fortunately Meg seemed not to notice her discomfort as Bill crouched down beside her.

'I've got something to tell you, Meg. I don't want to worry you, but I figured you would want to know, broken arm, or not.'

'Want to know what?' Meg asked. 'Who's ill?'

'No-one that I know of. It's about the site. There are rumours.'

'Is that all?' Meg said. 'You looked so solemn, I thought someone had died. There are always rumours. What is it this time?'

'Sounds a bit more serious than the usual tittle-tattle,' Bill said. 'There's talk of them building houses. Fred said he heard they were going to sell the land and turn us off.'

Amy was surprised when Meg laughed. 'Fred's always full of doom and gloom, bless him. He won't know any more than anyone else. I shouldn't worry about it too much.'

Amy hoped Meg was right and the talk of the sale of the land came to nothing. There would be a lot of very keen allotment holders who'd be very upset. It would be hard to find such a perfect spot anywhere else.

Later, when they walked back to the car, Meg admitted to feeling tired.

'If watching someone else gardening is enough to wear me out, it'll be some time before I can think of digging and planting myself,' she said. 'Though, if Bill's right, we'll all be turned off anyway.'

Meg's mood had plummeted - whether from tiredness, or from disquiet over Bill's remarks, Amy wasn't sure; but when they reached home, she suggested Meg have a rest.

'I'm going to have a sleep too,' she said. 'I'll come back later to cook our dinner.'

'Don't forget Mike's coming tomorrow,' Meg reminded her as she left. 'He's going to stay overnight. He says he's taking us both for a meal.'

17

Amy spent the next few hours wondering if she could get out of having a meal with Meg and Mike. She'd only half-promised him she would join them, if she wasn't working, but Meg was well aware her next shift was Sunday night. There was no logical reason for her to reject Mike's obviously friendly gesture. She could feign illness, but she saw so much of the real thing, that was something she wasn't prepared to do.

She didn't want to sit making small talk with him. She found his presence far too disturbing for that. Even the mention of his name set her nerves tingling. And Meg talked about him often. Her anecdotes about the past always seemed to include humorous stories about things Mike had said or done as a child. She would chatter on about how she hoped he got this job, and how lovely it would be to see him more often, while Amy struggled to keep her voice calm and respond non-committally.

She squared her shoulders and took a deep breath. A meal with Mike and his great-aunt was the ideal opportunity to establish a friendship where they both had Meg's interests at heart. Nothing more. She didn't want more. She had no intention of wanting more. Friendship. Full stop.

They probably had nothing in common, except their concern for Meg. And possibly a shared love of gardening. Hadn't Meg said he used to help her when he was a child? That he liked pattering about in mud. And maybe walking. She'd first met him when he was walking along the towpath.

So, apart from Meg, gardening and walking, she had no idea what interests they might share, and she had no intention of finding out. She was not going to allow anyone to get near to her again. Not after Justin.

She would suggest they went out for

lunch, and be polite and friendly. It was important to Meg she and Mike were civil with each other, but there was no need for more. He wouldn't be thinking of more. She wouldn't think about it again until tomorrow.

Except to decide what to wear. That wouldn't take long. Her wardrobe wasn't extensive, and it was only a casual lunch with her neighbour and a man she had no particular interest in. An hour later her bed was covered with discarded tops and skirts, jeans and trousers, as she searched in vain for the perfect combination. She might not be interested in Mike's approval, yet she didn't want to look dowdy.

Annoyed with herself, she finally selected a pair of grey trousers and a tunic top in soft greens and turquoises, and returned everything else to the wardrobe.

When Mike knocked the door next day all her good resolutions faded as she saw the approval in his eyes when she opened the door. If she had met him before Justin … but she hadn't. Her voice was calm and friendly, with no hint of her inner confusion, as she asked him to come inside while she fetched her coat.

'How has Aunt Meg been?' he asked. 'She says you've been very good to her. It's so kind of you.'

Amy reassured him that his aunt seemed to be recovering well, though there was a long way to go.

'She's really been looking forward to your visit,' she said. 'Her friends have been calling to see her, but she's so used to being out and about. I think she'll be getting very bored and fretful over the next few weeks.'

'We'll have to try to keep her spirits up,' he agreed. 'But apart from phone calls there's not a lot I'll be able to do. I need to work non-stop on my current project if it's to be finished on time. I don't know where I'll be after that.'

'You haven't heard about the job you applied for?'

'Not yet. They said it would be a while. They had others to interview.'

'It must be unsettling, waiting, not knowing where you'll be in a few weeks' time,' Amy sympathised.

Mike gave a rueful smile. 'That's why I'm so keen to work with this firm. It would mean I could settle in the area. I've spent the happiest times of my life here, with Aunt Meg.'

Amy remembered how she'd misjudged him, thinking he was bullying his aunt. Nothing could be further from the truth. He obviously cared for her deeply.

'Don't worry about Meg,' she said. 'Her arm is healing well. It's simply a matter of encouraging her to keep as active as possible, and not letting her get despondent when she can't do things. I took …'

About to say that she'd taken Meg to her allotment, and how much she had enjoyed the visit, Amy managed to stop herself in time. Meg might not have had time to tell him yet. It was best to keep off the subject.

Mike was looking at her, waiting for her to finish what she was about to say.

'I was just going to say I took her to the fracture clinic, but she'll have told you about that,' she finished lamely.

'Yes, she has. I'm so grateful to you, Amy. Shall we go? Aunt Meg is waiting.'

In the event, lunch was a jovial affair. Meg seemed to enjoy herself immensely, regaling them with tales of her travels, and scrapes she and her husband had got into when they were courting. And Mike had plenty of stories of his own to add.

Amy soon relaxed and began to enjoy herself. She hadn't laughed so much for ages, and was sorry when the meal came to an end.

'You must come back for coffee,' Mike said, as he paid the bill. 'Mustn't she, Aunt Meg?'

'Of course. You will, won't you, Amy? Mike makes a good cup of coffee.'

The quick cup of coffee Amy agreed to stretched well into the afternoon. As she sat quietly, listening to the banter between Mike and his aunt, she began to feel sleepy. It was difficult to adjust when she had a few days off in the middle of a stretch of night shifts, but she hadn't expected to feel comfortable enough in Mike's company to doze.

She had a hazy memory of her head being gently lifted and a cushion being placed under it, before she succumbed to sleep, and dreams where her relationship with Mike was very far from the cordial friendship she had been struggling to establish.

She woke to the sound of his voice, warm and full of humour, as he recounted the antics of his nephew to Meg. They were obviously a very close family. He and Meg were talking softly, taking care not to disturb her. She lay still for a while, reluctant to let go of her dreams and return to harsh reality, the real world where Mike must be kept at a distance.

She stirred, and he looked over at once, smiling gently.

There was no way he could have known what she had been thinking, but she felt herself blushing.

'I'm so sorry,' she stuttered. 'How rude. I should have gone straight home. I'll leave you in peace.'

'No need to go,' Mike protested.

'Thank you for a lovely meal, but I have things I need to do,' she said, embarrassment making her voice formal and distant.

18

The visit to Aunt Meg had gone well, Mike thought, as he drove back to Sheffield. Her arm seemed to be healing well, she was managing to look after herself, and Amy was there to give extra help and support where needed.

Amy … He'd enjoyed the time they'd spent together, though he hadn't managed to talk to her alone for more than the few minutes when he went to fetch her for their meal out. That meal had been fun. Aunt Meg had been on sparkling form, and Amy had listened and joined in with the conversation.

Always talking about things he or Aunt Meg had done, though. She was a good listener but he'd learnt little about her. She had moved to the cottage from a noisy rental in town, she was a nurse, but she hadn't worked at the local hospital long. This was a new job and a new area for her. That was all.

Whenever the conversation turned to her, she deftly turned it back. He didn't notice for a while, and he didn't think Aunt Meg had noticed at all, but Amy definitely didn't want to talk about herself.

And he minded. He wanted to get to know her. He wanted to know all about her. Was she in a relationship? Maybe with someone who was working away?

He'd asked Aunt Meg. She thought not. She thought Amy would have mentioned if there was a man in her life.

'She has talked about her parents,' Meg told him. 'But she doesn't talk about herself much. Anyway, what business is it of yours? Why do you want to know?'

Mike grinned, remembering the way she had peered at him through narrowed eyes.

'I'd like to get to know her better,' he admitted. 'But she doesn't seem interested. I thought it might be because she's already in a relationship. '

'Maybe she's just not attracted to you,'

Aunt Meg teased.

'Tell it how it is,' Mike grumbled. 'You're supposed to be on my side.'

'I am on your side, Mike. But I'm fond of Amy, too. I haven't known her long, but I wouldn't like to see her upset.'

'Why would I upset her? It's more likely to be her upsetting me.'

'You'd been with Emma a long time. She may want you back in her life.'

Mike had tried to convince Aunt Meg he and Emma were finished, even if things didn't work out with Eduardo. They might remain friends - probably would, they had a lot of mutual acquaintances. But they'd never be a couple again. He thought she was reassured.

'Anyway, what's wrong with taking things slowly? Like we used to do in the dark ages,' she teased. 'You'll be visiting again in a few weeks, you'll see her then.'

'I'd like to come earlier, Aunt Meg. But I have to finish this project on time. I'll be working all next weekend.'

'Don't worry. I'm doing well. You can see that I am. I know it's only concern

for me that has you so desperate to visit.'
She was laughing now.

'I'm glad I amuse you,' he grumbled.

'You're like a tonic, Mike. Don't be cross. Anyway, if you're so very worried, and you're not reassured by phoning me, why not phone Amy to ask her how I am?'

'What, talk about you behind your back?'

'Don't you do it all the time? You'll talk to your mother about me, why not Amy? Especially since it's my idea.'

'Aunt Meg, you're so devious!' He'd hugged her, and left, still chuckling.

By the time he reached home, he'd decided to wait until the following weekend, then phone Amy as Aunt Meg had suggested. That was reasonable. She couldn't object, as long as he kept the conversation firmly on his worries over her neighbour. Aunt Meg was right, there was no need to rush.

He submerged himself in his work. The contract was nearly finished, but he was still waiting to hear about the new job. He had no idea where he'd be, or what he'd be doing, in the next few months. He rang Aunt Meg, but managed to resist the urge to phone Amy for several days.

Then, one evening, after a particularly difficult day, he rang her number, apologised for disturbing her, and asked how she thought his aunt was managing.

'I'll be working every day for the next few weeks,' he said. 'But if you're worried and think I should come, I'll drive across after work. I've spoken to her, and she says she's doing well; but she would say that, wouldn't she?'

Amy reassured him, chatted for a while about the weather, promised to call him if she needed to. She sounded friendly, but a few bland comments about the rain and the first sprinkling of snow across the mountains hardly constituted a conversation. He reminded himself that he was going to take things slowly, as she finished the call, leaving him holding the phone, willing her to phone back.

When it did ring he almost dropped

it in surprise, but a quick look showed it was his sister.

'Lynda. How are you?' He settled back into the chair, thinking a chat with his sister about the latest activities of his young nephew would distract him from his confusion over Amy, but Lynda hadn't rung for a cosy chat.

'Mike, I need to talk to you. Emma's parents are worried about her. Can I come round?'

He agreed, but as she was driving the short distance from her house, he wondered irritably what on earth Emma's parents' worries were to do with him. It had been months since they parted, and it felt like longer. He wasn't interested.

'Sorry about this,' Lynda said as soon as she arrived. 'But Emma's parents are very anxious. They're talking of contacting the police. They haven't heard from her for weeks.'

'Mum told me about this last week,' he said. 'But I can't see why everyone's so concerned. Emma's an adult. She's gone off on a yacht with the love of her life.

She's hardly likely to phone home every five minutes. They're probably moored by some idyllic deserted island.'

'Possibly,' Lynda said. 'But apparently Emma had been keeping in touch, postcards mostly, letting them know where she was, or where they were sailing next, then nothing.'

'Probably no shops to buy cards,' Mike said, dryly. 'Highly likely there's no mobile contact either.'

'That's what I said. And if I had a chance to sail away I don't think I'd bother contacting civilisation frequently. But Emma's mother is really worried. She wanted me to ask you if you'd heard from her.'

'Why would I have heard?'

'Because ever since you were both children, she would call you if she was in any sort of trouble. Her mother thought she might contact you, out of habit. It seems reasonable.'

'It might seem reasonable, but I haven't heard anything. I've got enough on my mind winding up this contract, waiting to hear if I've got the new one, and everything else, without fretting about where Emma is. I honestly think her mother's fussing about nothing. She's as bad as Mum.'

'Not quite,' Lynda laughed. 'Mum said you told her Aunt Meg was recovering well. Is she? Or were you being overly optimistic to stop her worrying?'

'Aunt Meg was doing well when I went last weekend. I don't think there's any need for Mum to worry.'

'So what else are you worrying about?'

Mike frowned at his sister. 'What do you mean?'

'You just said you were worried about work and everything else.' Mike wasn't about to confide in his sister. It was enough that his great-aunt had lulled him into admitting his feelings for Amy; he didn't want more advice.

'I had been worried about Aunt Meg, but she's recovering, and being well looked after by her neighbour,' he said, then turned the conversation back to Emma's parents and their concerns.

'Emma's travelled a lot and worked abroad. There would often be spells when she'd be out of contact because one of us hadn't got reception. Her parents would be used to that. I wonder if there's something else worrying them they haven't told you. It seems odd that they're so anxious.'

They talked about other things for a while before Lynda went home, leaving him thinking about Emma's silence. She'd gone away with someone she hardly knew. It was unexpected, and completely out of character.

It was no wonder her parents were worried. He didn't like to think of them being so upset. They were nice people. They'd put up with him running in and out of their house for years, when he and Emma were at school. He'd promised Lynda he'd ring them, but when he did he learnt little more, except that Emma's mother didn't trust Eduardo.

'I thought you hadn't met him,' Mike said. 'Did he come over, or did you go to Lisbon?'

'We haven't met him. But Emma FaceTimed us, and we talked to him. She was at his villa, south of Lisbon. I didn't like him.'

'Difficult to judge from one conversation,' Mike said, thinking that she would naturally be anxious about this man, who had seemingly turned her daughter's settled world upside down. She'd still have been uneasy if Emma had fallen instantly in love with someone much nearer to home, as he had done with Amy.

'I know. And I was prepared to try to get on with him, for Emma's sake, but it was more than that. Ken said he didn't trust him. He was very agitated after the call. He's even more uneasy than I am.'

That did surprise Mike. Emma's father was the sort to think there was a rational explanation to everything. He promised to contact them if he heard anything, and spent the rest of the evening alternately thinking about Amy, and how to get to know her better, and Emma, and where she was. But when he eventually slept, it was Amy who filled his dreams.

19

Amy had returned to her cottage after their lunch, still embarrassed about falling asleep in Mike's company. She'd seen him briefly the next day when he knocked to leave his phone number before he drove home.

'In case you're worried about Aunt Meg,' he'd said. 'You can always get me on this number, even if you're just a little anxious. Don't worry, I won't tell my mother unless it's something serious. I'm a bit like Aunt Meg, I only tell Mum what I think she needs to know. It makes life much simpler.'

She'd wondered briefly what it was he'd been keeping from his mother, but it was none of her business. She gave him her number, so that he could phone if he was concerned, waved him goodbye, and tried to put him out of her mind. He'd been friendly, open, and easy to talk to.

That was all she wanted.

During her waking hours she almost managed to forget him; it was only when she was asleep that he invaded her dreams.

★ ★ ★

Over the following weeks he phoned several times. The first time she'd recognised his number she'd been wary, but he only wanted to know how his aunt was. He'd apologised for disturbing her and they'd had a friendly conversation.

When he called, several days later, again asking how Meg was, she told herself that this civilised friendship was exactly what she wanted. When he apologised for phoning, she assured him him he was welcome to contact her whenever he was concerned about his aunt.

She began to anticipate his calls and look forward to them. They started to talk of other things. She mentioned she went to the gym to unwind after a stressful shift at work, and how she was longing to go walking in the mountains.

He talked about the complications of his work, and how relieved he would be to finally complete the current contract. He told her about the times he spent with his sister and her family. There was no mention of a girl friend, and she began to think the girl in the photograph had simply been a friend, as Meg had implied.

Then he suggested they could go for a walk when he came next. For a brief moment she allowed herself to imagine rambling along the mountain paths with him, but she squashed the thought, before suggesting they should take Meg for a gentle stroll along the towpath, as long as the rain held off.

'She's been missing her walks,' she told him. 'I think we need to start encouraging her to do more and get her confidence back.'

★ ★ ★

Leaves were tumbling from the overhanging trees in ever-increasing numbers. The nights were drawing in, the season coming to an end, yet there was still plenty to do on Meg's allotment. When she'd taken Meg with her they'd gone in the car, but after her conversation with Mike, she suggested they should walk. The next time she had a few days off work, they set off wandering slowly along beside the river. Meg was delighted to be out walking and was full of chatter about what needed doing once they reached the plot and wondering who would be there. But she started apologising long before they reached the gate into the site.

'I'm slowing you up,' she muttered. 'It's not my leg I broke, but my feet don't seem to be as steady as they were.'

'Only because you haven't been walking much,' Amy said. 'We're in no hurry. Mike was saying maybe we could go for a walk together when he comes next.'

'So Mike's been phoning you?' Meg said, sounding pleased. 'Are you sure he meant me to come on this walk as well?'

Amy didn't think Meg would be pleased if she said Mike kept phoning to ask how well his aunt was managing.

'He was checking up on me, I suppose,' Meg said, when it became obvious Amy wasn't going to reply.

'He does always ask how you are,' Amy laughed. 'I tell him you're doing well.'

'Not as well as I'd like,' Meg grumbled as they reached the gate. By the time they were at the allotment she was looking exhausted, and Amy set out the garden chair, covered her legs with a blanket, and poured her a mug of tea from the flask she'd brought.

'Drink this,' she said. 'Have a rest and enjoy the view. You're bound to feel tired. It's a good walk, and you've been indoors for a while.'

'I've been going to the shop, and to the café,' Meg said.

'That's not nearly as far.'

'But I'm not going to be able to help you. I thought I could sort out the shed while you got on with the heavier things.'

'The shed doesn't need sorting,' Amy said. 'And it doesn't matter if we don't do any gardening. There's not much left to do. We came for the walk, really.'

Amy was concerned when Meg sounded so forlorn. She had always seemed brighter for a visit to her allotment, full of plans for the future and advice for Amy on what needed doing next. Now she was looking around almost with desperation.

'I've got to face it. I'm not going to be able to keep this on,' she sighed. 'It's not fair on you, Amy. You've got your own life to live.'

'What life?' Amy muttered, as she went into the shed to fetch the fork. 'I really don't mind,' she said, when she returned, 'I'm enjoying myself.'

'You don't mind now,' Meg said. 'But that's because you've only just moved in and you don't know many people. Before long you'll be meeting friends your own age and wanting to go out and about. You won't have time to be weeding an old lady's vegetable patch. And quite right too.'

'However many people I may meet, I'm sure I can find a slot in my hectic social life to walk up here once a week and keep things ticking over, 'Amy said. 'There won't be much to do all winter. By the time spring comes, you'll be back to your usual active life.'

'I hope so, but maybe Gwen's right, and I should cut down on my activities.'

'Didn't you say you were looking forward to going for walks with your group as soon as the strapping comes off your arm? You said they were planning some easier routes until you get your confidence back.'

'They are. But why should they do easy walks just because of me? I'm being a pain to everyone. Just what I said I'd never be. I wanted to be independent.'

Her voice wobbled and Amy was beside her in an instant, kneeling by the chair and taking her hands in hers.

'Don't you ever say you're a pain,' she said firmly. 'Everyone helps you because they want to ... '

'But I ... '

'You've been helping others enough for years. Now let them help you. I expect your friends will be only too glad to take more gentle walks for a change. They probably have a few aches and pains they're reluctant to admit to in front of such a feisty lady.'

'You could be right there,' Meg said, 'Emrys can still walk for miles, but a few of the others ask him to slow up occasionally. And our breaks to look at the view seem to have got steadily longer.'

'And as for me,' Amy insisted, 'I'm enjoying being allowed to come here on my days off. I've told you, it reminds me of happy times with my Granddad.'

20

Meg was still mithering about whether to renew the lease on the allotment when they walked slowly home. 'I think there's a list of people waiting for a space; it's not fair on them if I'm not cultivating mine properly. Though, if Bill's right and the site gets sold for building, the allotments won't be here for any of us.'

Amy worried that Meg was losing her fighting spirit, but a few days later she returned from work and found her neighbour unusually cheerful.

'Mike phoned this morning. He's got that job he's been waiting to hear about. He says he'll be starting in the New Year. He's going to rent somewhere near the site, but says he'll be able to visit often.'

She bustled off to put the kettle on, leaving Amy feeling a sharp pulse of excitement at the thought of Mike coming to live nearby. She'd spoken to him only last night, telling him about her concern over Meg.

'Her arm is recovering well,' she'd said. 'But she seems so low. She has friends call, and I've been seeing her as much as I can, but she keeps saying she's getting too old, and being a nuisance to people.'

Mike had told her his work was going well, and he should be able to come across the following weekend. He'd asked if she was working on the Sunday, said the weather forecast looked good, and suggested they could take Aunt Meg for a short walk.

She wanted to tell him how tired Meg had been after walking to her allotment, but she had promised not to mention her gardening exploits. She didn't want to deceive Mike; she didn't want to deceive anyone.

She'd finally told her mother that Meg was an octogenarian, and her mother, always ready to laugh at herself, had found it hilarious.

'You should have told me,' she'd said. 'You know you can tell me anything.'

Amy wondered if that was true. Could

she tell her mother about Justin? She had tried to lock the memories away, wipe him from her mind and start again. But it wasn't as simple as that. She had learnt not to trust anyone, had vowed never to let herself get close to another man, never to let a friendship develop into more. But the more she talked to Mike, the more doubts began to creep past her defences. Why did she constantly feel so guilty about her past relationship? What had she done wrong, except to trust the wrong person?

Why was she still letting Justin influence her life? She'd been in awe of him, flattered that he'd singled her out, overwhelmed by his attentions. She'd thought she loved him, but she'd never been able to relax when he was with her. He'd have been furious if she'd fallen asleep in his company, as she had done after her lunch with Mike and Meg.

For a moment she let herself remember when she first met Mike on the aqueduct, and her feeling of loss when she'd walked away. Before Justin, she'd have made time to talk to him, and skipped a meal to get to work on time. Before Justin, she'd have let the friendship develop.

Through university she'd had other boyfriends. Normal boyfriends. Did one mistake mean she should never love again?

Maybe simply telling her mother what had happened would help her see things more clearly. When she went home for Christmas there would be time to talk. Her mother had liked Justin on the one occasion they'd met. She might understand how easily Amy had been taken in

'Amy?' Meg said, calling her back to the present. 'I've brought you a cup of tea. Did you hear me say Mike's got the job?'

'Sorry, Meg. I was miles away. Thinking about something else. That's really good news. You must be so pleased.'

'I am. He heard this morning. He said he's coming to see me at the weekend, too. He's talking about us all going for a walk on Sunday.'

'Yes, he phoned me last night,' Amy admitted.

Meg grinned. 'So, was he checking up on me or finding an excuse to talk to you?'

'Did you ever get round to telling him about your vegetable growing?' Amy asked, knowing the answer, but determined to change the subject.

Meg wasn't to be deterred. 'So, are you coming out with us? I know you didn't have a great introduction to Mike, but that was as much my fault as his. We all had a good time when we went for lunch, didn't we?'

'We did,' Amy agreed. 'Until I fell asleep. I've already told Mike I'll come for a walk with you, but what about the gardening? I take it you haven't told him?'

'There's been no opportunity,' Meg said. 'What was I supposed to say when he was full of his news? 'Oh, by the way, I've not told you, I've been cultivating an allotment.' Why would he be interested? What has it got to do with his life and his plans? Besides, if I give up the lease he need never know.'

21

It was one of those rare clear November days. The tops of the mountains were sprinkled with snow, and the air was crisp and cold, but the sun shone. Just the day for a brisk walk, but Meg couldn't walk briskly.

Amy watched with amusement as Mike fussed, fastening her cloak firmly, making sure she had her gloves, a scarf and a woolly hat.

Meg became increasingly irritated and Amy began to suspect he was deliberately trying to annoy his aunt. Trying to provoke a reaction and spark her back into her usual spirited manner. Deliberate or not, it worked.

'Stop fussing, Mike,' she said. 'I can think for myself. And I can decide where to walk. I don't want to go along the towpath today.'

'We're not going on a trek up the

mountain,' Mike said.

'I agree,' Amy added, and felt her resolve to keep their relationship casual weaken as he smiled at her warmly.

'Gang up on me, why don't you?' Meg grumbled, but Amy could see she wasn't displeased. 'I want to walk along the river bank. There's no problem with that, is there?'

She looked at Amy, her eyes challenging. Amy wondered what she was up to, but could think of no reason to object, though she did wonder what would happen when they reached the allotments. Would they walk straight past without a word?

They paused frequently as they walked towards the river: people, out for a stroll, stopped to ask Meg how she was getting on.

'Aunt Meg seems to have plenty of friends,' Mike said, when he and Amy stood on the bridge waiting while Meg talked to a young family, who had been walking the other way.

'She does,' Amy agreed. 'Most days

she tells me about someone who's called to see her. She misses being out and about, though. She does walk to the nearest shop, but she feels uneasy going further, unless someone is with her.'

'This walk was a good idea,' he said. 'We'll have to do it more often.'

They stood side by side, leaning on the cold stone of the bridge, watching the antics of the canoeists on the river beneath. Amy was intensely aware of him. They were standing so close she could almost feel the warmth of his body. The urge to move her hand along the parapet to join his was almost impossible to resist.

'Sorry to keep you two waiting.'

Amy was relieved when Meg's voice broke into her wayward thoughts and they resumed their walk. She felt more composed with Meg walking between her and Mike, chatting to them both. Meg was walking much more confidently than she had a week ago when they'd come this way to her allotment.

They were already near the gate when

Meg tucked her arm firmly into Mike's and pulled him to a halt.

'Are you tired, Aunt Meg?' he asked, instantly concerned.

'I've got a confession to make, Mike.'

Amy couldn't avoid Mike's enquiring look, but she shrugged and said nothing, waiting to see what Meg would say.

'I'm going to tell you because Amy thinks I should. But it's my life, and whatever you say, I shall do what I want to do, and live it my own way.'

Mike was looking really concerned now, but Amy could see that he was listening carefully as she told him how much she had missed her gardening. She explained that she'd known she couldn't manage the huge garden she'd had, but she'd always grown things and she really missed it when she moved to the cottage. A few flowers and herbs in pots weren't enough.

As Meg talked, Amy saw Mike's sympathy grow.

'I'd not realised how much you missed it, Aunt Meg,' he said. 'All I could see was how good it was to get rid of the extra work.'

'The hedge-cutting and the lawn-mowing, yes,' Meg agreed. 'But I missed growing my vegetables. When spring came I was itching to start planting seeds. That first year in the cottage was the first time for over half a century I hadn't been eating my own radishes weeks before they appeared in the shops. I had to buy everything, and they didn't taste the same.'

'Nothing like a carrot straight from the soil,' Mike agreed.

'I brought you this way to show you something,' she said. 'You may not like it, Mike but I didn't want to give up gardening. I may have to soon. But it'll be my choice.'

She led the way through the gate and stood waiting while Mike looked around him. Amy closed the gate and followed as Meg led the way towards her plot. On such a pleasant day there were quite a few people working. Alicia left her fork and hurried across to ask

Meg how she was.

Amy saw the appreciative look in her eye as Meg introduced her to Mike and felt a pang of jealousy, instantly suppressed. If she only wanted to be friends with him, she couldn't object if other women showed an interest.

Wilfred was raking leaves. He asked how Meg was, nodded at Mike and Amy, and said his Rita was home with a cold so he wouldn't be staying long. Did she want anything doing before he left? Probably not, she'd obviously brought her helpers.

'This is my great-nephew,' Meg introduced Mike.

Wilfred shook hands then smiled at Amy.

'Hello, Amy. Nice to meet you again,' he said.

They walked on in silence. Amy had no idea what Mike was thinking, but he looked more amused than cross.

When they reached Meg's plot she produced the shed key from her handbag and asked Amy to set her chair out.

'I could do with a sit-down before we walk back,' she said. 'And I'm sure Mike's got plenty to say.'

'I usually bring a flask of tea,' Amy said, as Mike followed her to the shed. 'Your Aunt Meg sits and watches me work. I didn't know we were coming today.'

'You didn't think to tell me about this?' he said.

He sounded disappointed. As if she had let him down in some way. She supposed she had.

'It would have been a bit like telling on someone in the school playground,' she said. 'And Meg promised to tell you herself.'

He took her hand and gave it a gentle squeeze.

'Not to worry. This is fantastic,' he said, running his fingers over the neat shelves with the garden tools all set in their places ready for use. 'It's just like Aunt Meg used to have; though smaller, of course. How could I ever have thought she'd be happy without gardening?'

173

'Having an allotment is the perfect solution to you not having a vegetable garden, Aunt Meg,' he said, once she was settled in the chair. 'Once I start my new job I'll be able to lend a hand, if you'll let me. I don't suppose there's much left to do before the winter. If you had to break your arm, you chose the right time to do it.'

'Amy's been helping me,' Meg admitted. 'That's where she'd been when she came in and caught you shouting at me."

'So that's why you'd a basket full of veg,' Mike laughed. 'Why didn't you say?'

'Your aunt was telling me not to from behind your back,' Amy admitted, and burst out laughing. It was so silly, three grown-up people behaving like that.

'You won't tell your mother, will you, Mike?'

Mike looked at her, hesitated, then joined in Amy's laughter.

'I won't lie, but I won't mention it

unless the subject comes up,' Mike said. 'I see your point. She would definitely try to persuade you to stop, but I'd back you up and tell her she's wrong.'

They walked back shortly afterwards, stopping at Pete's café for tea and scones, before Meg gave Mike her walking stick to carry while she linked one arm through Mike's and the other though Amy's, and they strolled home.

It had been a good afternoon. Amy tried to think when she'd last been so contented. Certainly not since she met Justin, not since she left home for university to be honest. University had been fun, but frenetic at times, a mixture of hard work, new friends, exams and parties. She'd lost touch with all those friends. Justin had absorbed all her waking hours outside work, even when he wasn't with her. His work hours were long, and unpredictable. She worked shifts and kept all her spare time free in case he could see her. It was what he wanted and, thinking he was at work, she'd agreed, until gradually her friends and acquaintances drifted away.

Impatiently, she pushed thoughts of Justin away and remembered further back, to her childhood, to helping Granddad on his allotment. She was smiling again as Mike asked her to come for dinner, and said he was cooking. It was an offer she couldn't refuse.

His eyes met hers over his aunt's head, and even with Meg between them she was sure the strong feelings she had for him were reciprocated. If they'd been alone it would have been almost impossible to prevent herself from walking into his arms. Her hand was still tingling from when he had touched it reassuringly a few hours ago. She would have to be careful. She'd accept his offer, enjoy his company, but only because Meg would be there.

Over the next few weeks, as Mike's contract finished, he visited several times, always friendly, always trying to include Amy in whatever he and Meg were doing. What was at first an uneasy truce was developing into a warm friendship and, as she got to know him better, she relaxed a little. Maybe being taken in by Justin's duplicity was not entirely her fault. Dare she begin to hope for more than friendship from Mike? Dared she trust again?

He phoned her frequently, no longer making the excuse that he wanted to ask how Meg was. One evening, after a lengthy conversation, he asked if next time he visited she would go out for a meal with him.

'Just us,' he said. 'I'm sure Aunt Meg won't mind. I could take her somewhere in the daytime.'

She hesitated only a few seconds before accepting.

22

Mike was just leaving his flat, ready to drive to Aunt Meg's, when his mobile rang. Half expecting a nuisance call, he almost rejected it when he saw 'Number Not Available' on the display. He was startled to hear Emma's panicked voice.

'Mike. I'm in awful trouble. I don't know what to do.'

'Why? What's happened? Where are you?' he asked, as he put his overnight bag in the boot. He could hear her rapid breathing, and sensed that she was on the edge of panic. He sat in the car and put the key in the ignition, waiting to switch on the engine until she calmed enough to tell him what was wrong.

'Eduardo's gone. He sailed without me,' she said at last.

Mike drummed his fingers on the dashboard. What had this got to do with him? Emma had left him months ago.

'Why? Did you have an argument?' he said, trying to contain his impatience. She was obviously very distressed. 'Sort of. Mike, I'm stranded.'

'Where are you?'

'On an island called La Gomera. It's in the Canaries.'

'So book a flight and come home.'

'I can't. My bag's been stolen. I've no credit cards, and only the few euros that were in my pocket. My mobile's gone, too. I'm having to ring on the hotel phone.'

'What do the police say?'

'The police! I can't tell the police. You don't understand.'

He listened, alarmed, as she became increasingly distraught, saying Eduardo would kill her if she went to the police.

'How can he if he's not there?' Mike said, trying to sound calm and reasonable.

'You don't understand,' she repeated. 'He knows people. He'd find out.'

She sounded young and scared, like she had when she was eleven and was being bullied at school.

'Has he been threatening you?'

She didn't reply, but he could hear her muffled sobs and his irritation turned to sympathy. He was going to have to help her somehow.

'Do you have your passport?' he asked. 'Or was that in your handbag? If it was, you're going to have to report the loss to the police. You need to cancel your credit cards, too. You'll have to talk to the authorities, Emma.'

'I've got my passport,' she gulped. 'The hotel had it. But I've no money for food, and I can't pay for the ferry to the mainland.

'Please help me, Mike, I'm scared. There's no-one else I can trust. I don't know what to do.'

She was crying so much now he could hardly hear what she was saying. 'Give me the hotel number, so I can ring you back,' he said. It took several attempts, but once he had the number written down he told her to stay where she was, promising to phone back within the hour, when he'd worked out what to do.

'Don't tell Mum and Dad, please,' she pleaded. 'Don't tell anyone. Eduardo said I mustn't tell anyone.'

Mustn't tell anyone what? Mike thought, as he put his phone in his pocket, retrieved his holdall and went back into his flat. Emma was incoherent, panic-stricken and incapable of making sensible decisions. This wasn't the girl he'd known most of his life. He didn't love her, but he couldn't leave her in this mess, any more than he could ignore a plea for help from his sister.

There was a real edge of fear in her voice. Her parents should be dealing with this, but until he found out what that was going on, he decided to respect her wish not to tell them.

He needed to find out what had happened. The quickest way to do that was probably to go out there, deal with the situation and bring Emma home to her family. Decision made, he clicked into professional mode. This was no different to the many times he'd flown out to sort problems on projects he was managing. It took him little time to discover he needed to fly to Tenerife, then take a further flight to Gomera, or go on the ferry. Flying to Tenerife South and taking a taxi to the ferry seemed the easiest. He booked a flight for the following morning. Then rang Emma back to say when he would arrive.

'I'm coming over. I'll be there tomorrow,' he told her, cutting short her tearful thanks. 'Has the hotel got a restaurant? Have you eaten?'

'I couldn't eat a thing,' she sobbed. 'I don't want to leave my room. I feel safe here.'

He had been about to ask her to go to the reception and book him a room for a few nights, but decided to do it himself. It was simpler. He asked the name of the hotel and booked a room online while he was still trying to persuade her to eat something, then told her he'd be arriving next day on the evening ferry.

'Please don't tell anyone, Mike,' she begged.

'How am I supposed to explain my sudden disappearance?' he said.

'Please,' she cried. 'We could be back in Britain before anyone realises you've gone.'

'What makes you think no-one will miss me?' he snapped, stung by her easy assumption that he had not moved on with his life.

'I'm sorry,' she gulped. 'Mike, I'm so sorry. I didn't think. I'm just so frightened. I don't want anyone else involved. I'll explain when you get here, I promise.'

With Emma having a total meltdown, he felt pressurised into agreeing to keep silent.

He repacked his bag with clothes suitable for the warmth of the Canaries, put his passport and documentation together, and was ready to leave. It would have been better if he could have left at once. There was no time to get to Aunt Meg's, then back to the airport. Besides, he didn't want to talk to her before he'd seen Emma and assessed the situation. It sounded as if she was having some sort of breakdown. Surely Eduardo couldn't have sailed off and left her deliberately. Even if he was very angry and had sailed off, he'd be back for her next day, wouldn't he?

The Emma Mike knew wouldn't be stranded. She was no longer a bullied little girl. She'd grown into a resourceful adult. She'd held a responsible job. She'd have been furious, booked the first flight home, and never spoken to Eduardo again. Maybe he'd been trying to phone her, but couldn't because her mobile had been stolen. Why wouldn't she go to the police?

It didn't make sense. None of it made sense. But she was alone and terrified, and the sooner she was back with her parents the better.

For now, he needed to phone Aunt Meg, and give her some sort of explanation as to why he had to call off his trip to see her. An explanation that meant she would say nothing about it to his mother, if they happened to talk during the weekend. The fewer people who knew about this, the better, until he found out just what was going on.

For once, he was glad he wouldn't be able to speak to Amy. She would be at work. He couldn't tell her where he was going, or why he was postponing their date without breaking his promise to Emma – and even if he did tell her, what could he say? 'Sorry Amy, I'm flying off to the Canaries to rescue a former girl-friend who's in a bit of trouble'?

He groaned. It didn't sound good. The last thing he wanted to do was deceive her. It had taken so long, being patient and gaining her friendship. He'd been delighted when she'd agreed to go out with him. He'd booked a table at a restaurant in Llangollen and had been looking forward to it all week.

Aunt Meg had been delighted too, teasing him unmercifully when he'd told her his plans.

'So, let me get this straight,' she'd said. 'You're coming to see me, then leaving me alone while you take my next-door neighbour for a meal in a posh restaurant.'

'I'd better keep it simple,' he decided now. 'I'll tell Aunt Meg as little as possible, ask her to explain to Amy, and say I hope to be back by Monday, Tuesday at the latest.'

23

Meg wasn't concerned when Mike phoned. She'd have expected him to be on his way by now, but he'd obviously been held up and was phoning to say he'd be later than planned.

'Haven't you left yet?' she asked, before he could do more than say hello. 'I'll go on up to bed if you're going to be very late. I'll leave the key under the flower pot and you can let yourself in.'

He asked her how she was, and she could tell at once that something was troubling him.

'I'm fine,' she said, impatiently. 'What's wrong? Is it your grandmother? Is Lily ill?'

'Granny is much the same as usual,' Mike said. 'No-one's ill, but I'm sorry, I'm not going to be able to come tonight.'

'Will you come in the morning?' she asked.

Mike said he had to travel abroad suddenly, but he'd be back within a few days, and would come then.

'I've finished the contract, so I've no other commitments until I start my new job. My time's my own,' he said.

'I know that, Mike. That was why you were coming tomorrow, and hadn't planned exactly when you were going back to Sheffield. I assumed that was because you were hoping to persuade Amy into another date if your meal tomorrow night went well.'

'I really don't want to cancel, Aunt Meg. You know I don't. But I have to go and help a friend in trouble.'

Meg knew Mike too well not to realise he was very upset. 'What sort of trouble? Isn't there anyone else who can help?'

'Not really. I'm going first thing in the morning. Hopefully I'll be back on Monday. It'll depend on the situation when I get there.'

Meg thought for a moment. Something was very wrong. Who did Mike know that he would cancel his date with

Amy and rush off for? A colleague he'd met on contracts he'd done abroad? Unlikely. He'd have persuaded someone else to go, rather than risk upsetting Amy. This wasn't to do with work; it had to be more personal.

She remembered a previous occasion when he'd been visiting and had to rush off after a sudden phone call.

'It's Emma, isn't it?' she said. 'What's happened to her? Why can't her parents go? She's nothing to do with you any longer. You said you'd moved on. She left you for that Edmund, Eric – what was his name?'

'Eduardo,' Mike said. 'Aunt Meg, Mum's unlikely to phone because she thinks I'm with you, but if she does and she wants to speak to me, can you tell her I had to go off somewhere and I'll phone when I get back?'

'I'll not lie for you, Mike.'

'I'm not asking you to lie. I haven't told you anything except that I have to go to help a friend in trouble. Tell Mum that.'

'But is it Emma?'

'The less I say, the better. If Mum does phone, it'll make things easier for you.'

'Easier for you, you mean,' Meg said.

'I promise I'll tell you everything when I get back. My main worry is Amy.'

'I thought you'd forgotten about her.'

'Forgotten? Never! Trust me, if I could think of another way to sort this, I would. The last thing I want to do is let Amy down, but I think she'll understand when I explain. I hope she will. Will you tell her, Aunt Meg?'

'You want me to tell her you're not coming? Tell her yourself!' Meg was furious. What was the boy doing?

'I can't.' Mike sounded desperate now. 'She's at work all night. I can't ring her there. I'll be on the plane before she's off-duty. I thought maybe you could explain what's happened.'

'You haven't told me what's happened,' Meg sighed. Her flash of temper had fizzled out when she heard the distress in his voice. She agreed to talk to Amy, but she wasn't happy about it.

Long after Mike had rung off, she sat picking over what he had said, the few facts he'd given her going round and round in her mind, until she had a headache.

It had to be Emma he was rushing out to see. There was no other reason for him to want to keep it from his mother. She and Emma's parents knew each other quite well. Hadn't Gwen told him Emma's parents were worried about her? And Lynda had been asking if he'd heard from her. Mike had only seemed mildly concerned at the time, but were his feelings for Emma more complicated that he admitted?

If so, it was better his date with Amy was being postponed. Meg had become very fond of her and didn't want her upset.

What was Mike doing? It had taken weeks of quiet friendship before Amy had agreed to this meal with him. Was he risking everything because of a former girlfriend's escapades?

'Trust me,' he'd said. She hoped she could.

* * *

She had all night to fret about what she was going to tell Amy when she came home. She usually came to say hello after her night shift, and now that her arm was almost healed, Meg tried to repay her for all the meals she'd prepared over the past weeks by having breakfast ready if she wanted it. Though often a cup of tea and a piece of toast was all she'd accept before heading home for bed and a well-earned sleep.

Today she'd said she'd go straight home, as Mike would be there, and she'd see him later, after she'd slept.

'He said he'll wait for me to phone when I'm awake,' she'd said. 'We're going out about seven-thirty. I am looking forward to it, Meg. I haven't been out for ages, and your Mike is good company.'

Meg had known, or thought she'd known, how important this date was for Mike, but Amy had been much more cautious. So cautious that Meg wondered if she had been let down badly

192

in the past. Why else would the girl be so reluctant to date a man who she was obviously attracted to?

She put her mug of tea down, annoyed to see her hand was shaking. What she said about Mike's non-appearance might be important to whether Amy listened to his explanation, when he eventually gave it. The trouble was, she had so little information. She decided to keep to the few facts she did know, and not speculate on the rest.

She was an early riser, and she was waiting anxiously long before she heard Amy's car manoeuvring into place outside. She opened her door to call her in.

'Mike hasn't come,' she said. 'He phoned last night. Come in and I'll explain.'

'I spoke to him before I went to work last night, and he was almost ready to set off,' Amy said. 'Is someone ill? Not Lily, I hope.'

'No-one's ill,' Meg said. 'He's had to travel abroad at short notice, and as you were at work he couldn't phone you before he left for the airport. He'll be in the air by now.'

Meg watched as Amy's face reflected convicting emotions: confusion, disappointment, and finally resignation.

'Someone must have phoned between him calling me and his walking to the car,' she said. 'It must have been urgent. So where has he gone?'

'He didn't say. He says he hopes to be back Monday or Tuesday.'

'I expect he'll phone when he gets there.'

'I'm not sure,' Meg said. 'He said he had to go, but he'd be back as soon as he could, and talk to you then.'

'Something to do with work, I suppose,' Amy said. 'But I thought he'd finished working abroad. Did he really say nothing else? It all sounds very odd.'

Meg wished Mike hadn't told her he was going to help a friend in trouble. If he'd said nothing, she'd have assumed, like Amy, that it was something to do with a contract. Amy was frowning slightly, obviously trying to make sense of the situation. Should she tell her he'd said he'd gone to help someone? She decided not to say more. Mike shouldn't have put her in this situation. 'when she saw him, she'd tell him so.

There was an awkward silence, then Amy yawned, and stood up.

'Never mind, Meg. It was only a dinner, after all. You were looking forward to Mike's visit too. Shall I come round later and we'll plan something for us both to do tomorrow? Maybe we could do some Christmas shopping and treat ourselves to lunch out.'

Meg sat for ages after Amy had gone. She'd been expecting Mike to be there all weekend, chatting away about his date with Amy, asking if she needed shopping, telling her all the news from Sheffield. Now she would be spending the time worrying about his sudden trip. She'd be jumping every time the phone rang in case it was Mike's mother wanting to speak to him. Gwen was no more likely to accept Mike's thin explanation than she had done. She'd immediately think he'd gone looking for Emma, phone Emma's parents to see what they knew, and everything would escalate.

Having too much time alone to think was making her fret about things she could do nothing about. She needed company and no-one would call in to see her because all her friends thought she'd be spending the weekend with Mike. She couldn't ask anyone to come and visit without telling them Mike hadn't come. That would mean more evasions and half-truths. Muttering crossly about her great-nephew, she reached for her cloak and walking stick and set off for a walk.

24

In spite of her exhaustion, Amy found it difficult to sleep. She'd put up thick curtains, with lightproof linings, in her bedroom, so the room was as dark as if it were night. There was no sound from outside. The bed was warm and comfortable, but she'd been expecting to fall asleep thinking of seeing Mike that evening. She'd bought a new dress. It was hanging in the wardrobe, waiting.

This was the first time she'd dated since her break with Justin. It was important to her, though all week she'd been reminding herself it was simply a meal out.

Obviously it hadn't been so important to him. Which was a good thing, wasn't it? After all, she didn't want a deep relationship, did she? She wanted a warm friendship. And if a friend needed to travel abroad suddenly, and had to call off a previous arrangement, there was no need to feel devastated, was there?

Her feelings were a warning that she mustn't let herself get too involved with Mike. She couldn't trust herself.

It was odd that he hadn't promised to ring her as soon as he arrived. Maybe he didn't know what the situation would be when he got there, wherever he was going.

She replayed her conversation with Meg as she finally drifted off to sleep, then jerked awake again. Meg hadn't said he'd gone abroad for work, had she? She had surmised he had, and Meg hadn't commented. Hadn't his last contract abroad been in Latin America? She was sure he'd talked about being in Belize. If there were problems there, he wouldn't have been talking about being back by Tuesday. It would probably take until then for him to arrive.

Was he in some sort of trouble? Amy had an uneasy feeling Meg knew more than she was saying. Her neighbour had seemed unusually tense as they were talking.

She woke several times during the day, jolting into reality from surreal dreams. Nightmares where Mike was always involved in bizarre dangerous situations which she was forced to watch without being able to intervene to help. Eventually she gave up even trying to sleep. It had been her last night at work for some time. She had a few days off now, then would be back on day shifts for a while.

She showered and dressed, then wandered aimlessly around the cottage, feeling thoroughly miserable and angry with herself. She'd vowed never to let a man disturb her sleep again. She would keep her distance from now on. She could avoid him when he came to visit Meg. It was perfectly possible. It was fortunate he'd broken their date. It showed how she'd let her feelings take over her common sense. It was a warning. She wouldn't let it happen again.

When he sorted out his problem and came to stay with Meg, she would be at work most of the time. She'd plan a few evenings out. The other nurses always invited her when they went out together. They were going for a meal on Monday night to celebrate Sally's birthday. As usual, she'd refused, but she could change her mind.

There was a Christmas party being planned, too; she ought to go to that. But, even as she thought it, she knew she wouldn't go. It was at a party after work that she'd first met Justin. He'd recently started working at the hospital where she'd been since she left University. No-one knew much about him. He'd looked lost, and she'd felt sorry for him, not knowing it was his well-rehearsed way of reeling in his latest potential conquest.

She shivered and reached to turn the heating up. She was looking forward to Christmas and getting away for a few days. It was the first year for a long time that she had enough time off over the holiday to go home. Though she was working on Christmas Day, she would finish by early afternoon, drive straight to the Lake District, and be there in time for Christmas dinner with her parents in the evening.

Her siblings wouldn't be there this year, just herself and her parents. It would be the ideal time to finally talk to them about why she had parted with Justin. She'd allowed them to go on thinking he was wonderful for far too long. She needed them to know the truth.

Still restless, she pulled on her coat and went to see if Meg wanted to come out for a meal with her, but mainly to see if she had heard any more from Mike.

She hadn't. Amy was concerned to find Meg slumped in her chair, looking completely exhausted.

'Whatever's happened?' she asked. 'Have you heard from Mike? Is he all right?'

'I haven't heard. I've been out for a few hours. I was restless, so I took myself for a walk along the towpath, and went further than I intended to.'

'Should you be walking on your own, yet?' Amy asked.

'Probably not, but I had my mobile,

and the canal towpath is easy walking. I was going to climb up the mountain, since Mike isn't here to object, but thought that would be a bit much,' Meg teased, trying to lighten the mood.

'I expect he'll phone me soon,' Amy said. 'He knows I won't be at work.'

'I don't think we'll hear until he's back,' Meg said.

'Why not? I don't see why he couldn't phone this evening. It wouldn't take many minutes to call and apologise. Whatever the crisis is, he'll have to stop working to eat.'

'But he's not working. He's gone to ...' Meg stopped suddenly, her hand across her mouth, like a child caught telling a secret.

Amy stared at her. Meg knew more than she was saying. Mike hadn't gone to sort out a problem with work. So where had he gone? And why was Meg being so cagey about it? Had Mike told her not to say what he was doing, and if so why?

'I thought you said he'd gone to sort

out a problem,' she said. 'I assumed it was work.'

'No, not work. A friend of his was in trouble, and he's gone to help them.'

'What sort of trouble? Didn't he say where he was going? Who is this friend?' The questions came thick and fast. She had been quick to decide to keep her distance from Mike, quick to interpret his sudden trip abroad as a reason not to get involved with him, but if he'd gone to help a friend that was different.

Meg was wringing her hands together, obviously distressed. Amy sat beside her and spoke more gently. 'It seems so odd, Meg. Don't you think? Did he say nothing to give you a clue where he was going? Is he in any danger?'

'Danger? I don't think so, he seemed to think he could sort things out and bring the friend home. And he was talking of being back by Monday, so wherever he's gone it's not Australia or South America,' she said, attempting to laugh.

'If he's bringing his friend home, it must be someone he knows well,' Amy said. 'You've no idea who this friend is?'

'He didn't tell me,' Meg said, getting out of her chair and heading for the kitchen. 'I'll put the kettle on.'

He might have not told her, but Amy thought Meg had a good idea who he'd gone rushing off to Europe for, and Amy did, too. In one of their rambling telephone conversations, Mike had told her about his long relationship with his childhood sweetheart. She had felt guilty at the time because she hadn't even mentioned Justin, but she was used to feeling guilty, she'd felt guilty ever since she'd found out about his treachery.

Mike had been sure he'd moved on, and had told her he wasn't in the least distressed. But had he been deluding himself? Had he gone running at the first sign his ex was in some sort of trouble? Did Meg suspect that was the case? Was she uneasy because she was afraid Amy would be upset?

She decided to tackle the problem head-on.

'You know, I think he's gone to help

that childhood sweetheart of his, I forget her name. She's clicked her fingers and he's gone running. She's probably had a row with the Portuguese boyfriend.'

'Emma,' Meg said. 'Her name was Emma. He's told you about her, then?'

'Only that they'd known each other for years, and that she'd fallen for someone she met in Lisbon. Do you think she's had an argument with this new man, and Mike's gone to console her? If she rang in tears he may have realised he minded their break-up much more than he had thought. He might have been too embarrassed to admit it.'

Meg didn't reply, and Amy took her silence for agreement.

'You know, he really didn't need to worry, Meg. He could have just said where he was going, you could have told me. I'd have understood. It's not as if Mike and I are romantically involved. We're simply friends who were going out for a meal together. I think he wanted to thank me for looking after you, though he didn't need to. I've been glad to help, and I enjoy our friendship.'

'It may not be Emma who rang him, and if it was, the trouble she was in must have been far more than a simple falling-out with Eduardo. Mike felt there was no alternative but to go and help. And I'm sure he thinks of you as more than a friend,' Meg protested.

But Amy was sure her own interpretation was correct. Mike would phone to say he was home, and that he and Emma were back together. She would say she was pleased for him. She would hide the fact that inside she was devastated, that her stomach was churning, that she felt she was falling down a long, icy tunnel with no sign of an end. Given the strength of her reaction, it was fortunate the knowledge had come now. If she felt this way before they'd even been on a date, or kissed, how would she have felt if he'd found out he still loved Emma after a few months?

She squared her shoulders and pinned a smile on her face. It was only a date; anything more had been only in her imagination. He'd promised her nothing. There was no need for Meg, or Mike, to ever know how upset she was. Mike would be too busy with Emma to visit his aunt often. Amy was determined not to let this come between her and her friendship with her neighbour.

'Right, Meg,' she said. 'Mike isn't coming, so we'll have to entertain ourselves. How about we drive into Chester tomorrow? The shops will all be decorated for Christmas. We could shop a little, and then treat ourselves to lunch out.'

25

After ringing his aunt, there had been nothing for Mike to do but try to rest before leaving for the airport at about three in the morning. He desperately wanted to talk to Amy, but she'd be working all night. He wondered how she coped with her changing shifts.

He couldn't settle. He should have been on his way to Hen Bont, not spending the evening alone in his flat. He decided to ignore the landline if it rang — unless it was Aunt Meg. His mother knew he was going away for the weekend, but was likely to forget when he was actually planning to leave, and phone with some last-minute message.

He didn't want her to find out he'd gone abroad until he was back home. If Emma's parents thought he'd heard from her, they'd be straight round to his flat and insist on coming with him. Mike would have been grateful for her father's company, but he'd promised Emma not to tell them. Best to get her home as quickly as possible. The questions and recriminations could take place once she was safe.

The calm, assured, confident woman she had become seemed to have reverted to the frightened, bullied, child he'd first known.

He knew little about Eduardo, but something he had said or done had obviously terrified her. Now he'd disappeared from the scene, leaving her alone. There was no point speculating further: tomorrow evening he'd be with her and learn the truth. Hopefully he could persuade her to phone her parents straight away, but whatever she said, they'd be on the next available flight home.

If only Emma's crisis had happened a few days later. If she'd called when he was with Amy, they could have talked about it. Amy would have seen that he needed to go. He knew she would. She would have understood that Emma was just a friend in trouble, and not a threat.

Mike had been pacing around the flat, too restless to stay in one place. He stopped suddenly, staring out of the window. A threat? A threat to what? He knew Amy was the person he wanted to spend the rest of his life with. He knew how he felt about her. But he had no idea what her feelings were. Far from seeing Emma as a threat, she might not even be concerned.

After their shaky start, he'd spent weeks trying to get to know her. Weeks of casual phone calls, shared meals with Aunt Meg, time spent together on the allotment, with his aunt sitting in her chair watching them like a chaperone. Amy had seemed happy to have it that way, showing no sign that she wanted any more than friendship. Had he imagined that sometimes, when their eyes met, his interest was reciprocated? If their hands brushed accidentally, he'd almost persuaded himself his longing to hold her in his arms was mutual.

Their phone calls had become longer,

rambling over so many subjects. He'd told her about Emma, but she'd not mentioned previous relationships herself. If there was someone, surely she would have said? She must know how he felt about her.

He'd been watching the traffic speeding past on the distant motorway. The roads would be much quieter when he drove across to Manchester in the middle of the night. There should be no hold-ups. He checked the online traffic report for road works. Nothing that would affect him, but there was a weather warning for ice. He set his alarm for an hour earlier than he had intended, and went to bed. He was used to snatching sleep at odd hours, when travelling for work, and slept deeply, waking with a start when the alarm sounded a few hours later. Time to leave.

It had been frosty overnight and, as forecast, the roads were icy. Driving was slow and treacherous until he reached the motorway, but the gritting lorries had been out. He put the car's heating on full and concentrated on the road as he drove to the airport, arriving with no time to spare before joining the queues for security. He left Britain without the substantial breakfast he'd promised himself, and slept for most of the flight.

By early afternoon he was stepping out of the airport at Tenerife into the bright warmth of November in the Canary Islands. The next ferry for La Gomera didn't leave for several hours, so there was plenty of time to take a taxi to Los Christianos and have a leisurely meal before walking across to the ferry terminal. Not that he wanted to relax in the sunshine. He wanted to get over to the island, talk to Emma, and book their flight home. He felt totally incongruous amongst the clusters of holidaymakers strolling around in shorts and T-shirts, laughing and chattering.

He'd already found there was no flight available Sunday, but there were seats on a flight just after two pm on Monday. He had every intention of being on that plane. Emma could be home with her parents Monday evening.

He watched a couple walking along the sand, hand in hand, and wished Amy were with him, but resisted the urge to phone her. She might be asleep, and what could he say? 'I broke our first proper date to fly to help my ex girlfriend, who'd got herself in some sort of trouble'?

It didn't sound good, however he phrased it. He needed to tell her the whole story, and apologise in person.

He phoned Emma instead, told her what time the ferry would arrive, and asked directions to the hotel. She told him it was within walking distance of the harbour, but refused to come to meet him.

'I can't, Mike,' she said tearfully. 'It'll be dark by then.'

Emma had never been afraid of the dark. She was obviously on the verge of panic.

'Have you left the hotel at all since we spoke yesterday evening?' he asked.

'I haven't been out of my room, except for breakfast,' she said.

Mike frowned. He had hoped her panic would have subsided by now, that she would have reported the theft of her handbag to the police, and be feeling embarrassed that she'd been in such a state when she called him. Instead, she sounded even more upset than she had last night.

'As soon as I get there, you can tell me exactly what's been going on,' he said. 'Then I'll arrange flights and get you home.'

The ferry trip was uneventful. It was a pity it was dark, but he stood on the deck watching as the lights of the tiny town of San Sebastian drew nearer. Another time, in other circumstances, it would have been a magical experience.

He wished he could be visiting for a different reason. He'd spent part of the previous evening reading a little about the island, and longed to be able to don his walking boots and set off on one of the many trails described. A walker's paradise, they'd called it. He wanted Amy with him. They could wander along the paths up the barrancos, past the tiny terraced fields, into the laurisilva forests.

He'd tell her about it and bring her one day. She'd understand about Emma. He was sure she would. She must know how he felt about her.

The ferry entered the sheltered harbour and manoeuvred into place alongside the jetty. He joined the group of foot passengers waiting to disembark and watched the gangplank being lowered. The gate was opened, and they streamed off, Mike amongst them.

Emma's directions to the hotel were clear. He passed the waiting taxis and was crossing in front of the terminal building when she emerged from the shadows and threw herself into his arms.

'Mike, I'm so glad to see you. You've no idea.'

He disentangled himself and looked at her careworn face. Her eyes were darting about, looking over his shoulder, left and right, watching, wide with terror.

'I thought you were staying at the hotel,' he said. 'Let's get a taxi.'

'No. It's not far.' She led him along the road towards the harbour entrance. 'And the driver might know Eduardo.'

'Why would he?' Mike was mystified. What was going on?

'We can walk and talk on the way,' she said, as they left the lights of the harbour behind them, but in spite of her promise to talk, she remained silent, clutching his arm as they climbed up a steep, narrow, camino towards a small pension perched above the harbour.

26

'I'll go ahead,' Emma said, as they neared the pension. 'The fewer people who know we're together, the better.'

'We're not together,' Mike muttered, as she loosened her tight grip on his arm.

She ignored his comment. Mike wasn't sure if she'd even heard him.

'I'm in room eight. Come when you've checked in.'

He watched as she scurried ahead and turned into the entrance, her furtive manner marking her out far more than if she had calmly walked in chatting to him. He looked around himself, wondering if he was being watched, then shrugged his shoulders. There was no-one. Why should there be? He had no connection with anyone on the island, except Emma, and she had obviously told no-one he was coming. He mustn't let her fears affect him.

What had Eduardo said or done to cause such panic? The sooner she started talking, the better. He needed to get her home to her family. Now he'd seen her, he wished he'd spoken to them. She needed her mother.

The hotel lobby was welcoming but Emma was nowhere to be seen. He was shown to his room, which looked out over the harbour, far below. The last few vehicles were leaving, the town was quiet. He turned back to the room, and phoned Emma.

'I'm coming now,' he said. 'And I want explanations.'

She opened the door before he could knock, and pulled him inside after a swift glance up and down the corridor.

'Did anyone see you coming?' she said.

'There was no-one around. Not outside my room, not as I came down the stairs, not as I came along this corridor. no-one was watching me. Emma, what is all this about?'

He sat heavily on the only chair in the room, leaving her to perch on the side

218

of the bed, chewing at the ends of her hair and staring at him with those huge deep brown eyes that had captivated him when they were little more than children. Not any more!

'You're angry with me,' she said. 'I don't blame you. I'm angry with myself.'

'I'm not angry. I'm confused and irritated, because you're not making sense. Start at the beginning. You said Eduardo sailed without you. Why?'

'We were staying at the Parador for a few nights,' she said. 'One of his crew came to talk to him. He told me to go onto the balcony while they talked.'

'Told you!' Mike said, raising his eyebrows. She ignored him and carried on talking in a flat voice.

'A few minutes later I heard the roorn door close and he came out and told me we had to leave. We would be sailing on the next tide. We had an argument. I walked off, in a temper. When I came back, he'd gone. The receptionist told me he'd settled the bill and left a note for me. It said the yacht would be sailing

219

in a few hours. If I wasn't there, they'd go without me.'

Mike had been watching her face as she talked. She'd told him as little as possible.

'That's not good enough,' he said. 'I've come all this way because you said you were in desperate trouble, and that's all the explanation I get? Did you go to the harbour? Why would he sail without you? I thought he was supposed to be in love with you. Why would he leave you? Emma, talk to me. There must be more to it than a lovers' squabble.'

She began rocking frorn side to side, shaking her head. He crossed to the bed, sat beside her and took her hand.

'Emma. Look at me.'

She looked up at him, her eyes fearful, and full of tears.

'If you don't tell me what's really going on, how can I start to help?' he said.

'Eduardo warned me not to tell.'

'He'd no right. Everyone needs someone to talk to.' She leaned her head on his shoulder and he hugged her.

'Corne on. Tell Uncle Mike.'

She giggled, slightly hysterically.

'I've been anxious for some time,' she said. 'At first, everything was wonderful. We sailed to so many places.'

'I know,' Mike said. 'Your mother showed Lynda the postcards you sent. Then you stopped communicating with your parents. Why? You must have known they'd be concerned.'

'Things got complicated. I met his family on their farm in the Alentejo. His father was a big, burly man, didn't say much, and didn't seem pleased to have me there. His mother was very welcoming, though she spoke no English, and my Portuguese is very limited, so we couldn't talk much. They seemed to run some sort of business alongside the farming, but I'd no idea what. We didn't stay long.'

'You weren't curious?' Mike said, removing his arm from her shoulder.

'Not at the time, but later, as we sailed from place to place, I overheard snippets of conversations, and began to get apprehensive. Eduardo often set up meetings with people and gave me money to go off and enjoy myself. I was never introduced to any of his colleagues. Whatever his business was, it was very secretive. When we were sailing here from Madeira, I asked him how he earned his money. At first he was dismissive. He told me not to worry my head about that sort of thing.'

Mike wondered how she'd responded to that comment, but now that she was finally talking, he didn't want to interrupt.

'I persisted, told him about things I'd overheard, or deduced as we'd sailed from place to place. He became very agitated. He wanted to know just what I was accusing him of. I hadn't been accusing him of anything; I only had vague suspicions, nothing that really made sense.

'He said it was none of my business how he earned his money, and that I was happy enough to enjoy the rewards. He turned really nasty, cold and menacing. He warned me not to talk to anyone about his work, or I'd regret it.

'We were heading for the Canaries, I assumed Tenerife, and I was considering leaving him and flying home from there, but we sailed to La Gomera. As we anchored in the harbour at San Sebastian, he changed again and became the attentive, caring person I'd fallen in love with. He apologised for his temper, said we needed some time to ourselves away from the ship, and booked a room at the Parador.'

'Money no problem, then,' Mike commentated dryly.

Emma continued her story, giving no sign she had heard him.

'I was still concerned. He hadn't explained away my unease, and if he had nothing to hide, why had he become threatening? Once we booked into our room, I told him that unless he could convince me his business was legal, I would leave him.

'He tried to convince me there was nothing to worry about, but we were interrupted by someone who wanted to speak to him urgently. I was sent onto the balcony while they talked. I heard whispering, then the man left and Eduardo came out to say we were returning to the ship.

'I said maybe he should go without me. He said since I didn't trust him, that was probably a good idea. I stormed off into the grounds. When I got back, he was gone.'

'You didn't try to follow him?'

'I'd had enough. I packed my holdall and took a taxi into town. If the yacht was still in harbour, I intended to tell Eduardo my decision, and say goodbye. But he'd sailed without me; and, to be honest, I was relieved.'

'So why the panic?' Mike asked. 'You'd decided to leave him. He'd gone. Why not just book a flight and go home?'

'It was too late for me to travel until next day. I booked into this small hotel, and then went for a meal in town. Afterwards, I sat watching the ships in the harbour, wondering where Eduardo was going, and what had made him sail so suddenly. I was sure he'd wanted me to go with him – but was that because he loved me, or because he was afraid of what I might say to others?

'Then my bag was stolen. I was going to report it, then I began to worry that the man who'd come to talk to Eduardo might be watching me.'

'Why would he be?' Mike interrupted.

'I thought Eduardo might have told people he knew here to watch me. If they saw me talking to the authorities, they'd think I was telling them …'

'Telling them what!' Mike shouted, exasperated.

'I think Eduardo was part of a drug-smuggling gang,' she whispered. 'I think his father and brothers were involved, too.'

Mike didn't know what to think. No wonder Emma was frightened, but she had no facts to back up her suspicions. Eduardo had certainly left in a hurry. Had he been brought news that forced him to alter his plans?

It seemed unlikely he'd have told any-one to watch her, but if he had, they wouldn't have drawn attention to themselves by stealing her handbag. That was the work of an opportunistic thief taking advantage of her preoccupation and inattention.

He could understand her reluctance to report it, though. She didn't want to draw attention to herself by walking into a police station.

'Can I see the note Eduardo left you?' he asked.

She pulled it out of her pocket and handed it over. As he read, Mike could see why Emma was nervous. The note said he had to sail immediately, and when she thought about him, or mentioned him to others, she must only remember the good times they'd enjoyed together.

Nothing threatening about it. But anyone who hadn't heard Emma's suspicions wouldn't notice the subtle threat that his underlining of the word 'must' conveyed. She'd been concerned, but she'd found a quiet hotel and was making plans to return home. It was only when she lost her money that her situation seemed precarious, and she'd panicked and called him.

'There's no flights tomorrow,' he said, as he opened his laptop and logged on. 'I'll see if we can still get seats on the afternoon flight from Tenerife on Monday. We can take the morning ferry.'

Emma sat chewing her nails as he booked tickets.

'Now, I suggest you try to sleep,' he said. 'Maybe tomorrow we can see a bit of the island. I'll hire a car.'

He returned to his room, still thinking over her story. She had to be overreacting, didn't she? Eduardo's note was written in a hurry. It could be interpreted differently, depending on your point of view. If he thought he was being investigated for something, he might want to keep Emma out of any trouble. He might be relieved she wasn't on the yacht.

She didn't really seem to know anything concrete. Her fears were all based on suspicions. Eduardo's family might simply be private about their business dealings, not wanting competitors to gain an advantage. They hardly knew his new girlfriend. They wouldn't confide in her.

But, before she met Eduardo, Emma had always had good judgement. If she thought there was something illegal going on, she was probably right. It was for her to decide what, if anything, she should do next. His responsibility would end when he got her home.

27

Meg was listening to the radio as she made her porridge and toast on Sunday morning. Getting her breakfast was slow, but she didn't need Amy's help any longer.

The news was dominated by reports of the first snowfall of the winter.

'What's news about snow on the mountains in December?' she grumbled, as she waited for the kettle to boil.

She was looking forward to the trip into Chester and didn't want it cancelled because of dangerous roads. She peered through the window into her back yard. The ground was thick with frost but the weather locally promised to be clear and sunny.

Amy needed a day out, too, she thought as she cleared up. For an instant yesterday, her face had reflected how disappointed she was that Mike wasn't coming. She'd covered her dismay quickly, but when he did finally arrive he was going to need a really good explanation if she was to agree to another date.

She was ready and waiting when Amy knocked the door and came in.

'Lovely morning, Meg, but cold. You'll need your hat and gloves.'

'Are the roads icy? Are you sure you want to drive?'

'There's no problem going to Chester. The Christmas market is open. Have you ever been?'

'I haven't,' Meg said, determined to enjoy herself, even if Mike wasn't there. 'It should be fun. I'm hoping to buy some presents.'

'We could go early evening when all the lights will be on, if you want to get the full atmosphere.'

Meg laughed. 'I think we'd be better imagining the scene after dark, rather than experiencing it. You could go one evening with your friends from work.'

'I might do that. In fact, I was thinking of going out straight from work tomorrow evening, though not to the Christmas market. Could you manage?'

'Of course I can manage. You've been waiting on me long enough. Besides, Mike might come.'

'I shouldn't think so,' Amy said. 'It will depend on how much help his friend needs. But if you're sure you don't mind being on your own, a friend at work is celebrating her birthday and I've been invited to a meal with her and a few colleagues.'

'You go,' Meg said. 'I'll be seeing Madge in the afternoon, and I'm well able to cook for myself now, if I take it slowly.'

'I thought it was time I took your advice and went out more.'

Meg was thinking about Mike as they drove into Chester. Where was he? Would he be home tomorrow? Why didn't he phone?

She needed to put him out of her mind for a few hours. There was nothing she could do until she had more information.

'When we get there, I'll treat us both to an early lunch,' she said. 'Then I have a list of things I want to look for. I want some mulled wine to take to Sheffield with me at Christmas. Do you think we can sample it? Or is that only later in the evening?'

'I'm sure you can sample it,' Amy laughed. 'I can't, I'm driving. Are you going to stay with Gwen over the holiday?'

'I've promised to stay for a few weeks and see the New Year in with Lily,' Meg said. 'Mike is coming to fetch me on Christmas Eve.'

She sighed heavily. Having decided not to think about him, she was mentioning him in her next sentence.

'Don't worry about Mike,' Amy said. 'I'm sure he'll turn up someday soon, full of apologies. We're going to enjoy ourselves. I've got things I want to buy, too. I'm going home for a few days at Christmas this year. I want some fudge for Mum, and maybe I'll find something quirky for Dad. Oh, and I want some carved decorations for the Christmas tree. I always take something to add to the box Mum has collected over the years.'

Meg told Amy about her own box of decorations, saved from her childhood.

'My father was away in the war, but Mum always made an effort to make Christmas special for me and Lily. It was the same for all the families in our street, of course. We had a party at Sunday school, jelly and blancmange, Spam sandwiches, and little cakes. I buy a small tree every year and remember those times when I put the decorations on it.'

Over lunch, they chatted about their plans for Christmas, then joined the cheerful crowds wandering along the streets, in and out of shops, and around the market stalls.

Families were out taking advantage of the sunny afternoon. The children's faces were overjoyed as they gazed at the piles of toys, the trays of sweets, the candyfloss, and the sparkling lights everywhere.

The pungent smell of spices filled the air from a myriad of food stalls offering everything from beefburgers to German sausages. Meg sampled the mulled wine, before buying a bottle to take to Gwen, and was so enthusiastic about it that Amy bought one for herself.

A choir was singing Christmas carols outside the cathedral. As they stood, listening to the well-known favourites, Meg felt tears pricking the back of her eyes, remembering Christmases when she and Lily had been children. They hadn't had much in terms of money, but they'd had a loving home. How much of that time did Lily remember?

'It'll be good to spend time with my sister,' she told Amy. 'We were always very close.'

The temperature dropped sharply as the sun began to set. Meg shivered and pulled her cloak closer around her.

'Time we were heading home,' Amy said.

The Christmas lights were sparkling in the twilight as they wandered back through the town towards the car park. They could still hear the carol singing, the music hanging in the frosty air.

Meg strolled along beside Amy, who was laden down with shopping bags.

'I shouldn't have bought so much. I forgot I couldn't carry it,' she said.

'Half of this is mine. I think our day has been a success, don't you?'

'Magical,' Meg said. 'Thank you. It was a good idea for us to get out.'

They didn't talk much on the way home. Meg was tired and closed her eyes as Amy drove, only waking when the car stopped outside the cottages. She allowed Amy to carry her shopping indoors, but refused when she offered to make her a cup of tea.

'You get on home and unpack your own shopping,' she said. 'We've had a lovely day, but now I'm going to rest.'

Amy left, promising to call before she left for work next morning, and Meg sighed with relief as she removed her shoes and slipped her feet into her comfy slippers.

She saw the message light flashing on the phone as she walked through the living room, but ignored it until she'd made herself a cup of tea and cut a slice of cake.

When she eventually sat down and picked up the phone she found two messages. The first from Mike, saying he would be returning to Britain on Monday evening, and would drive over on Tuesday morning. He asked if she could tell Amy. That was a message that could wait until the following morning. At least they knew when he would be home.

The second message was from Bill. He said he was thinking of setting up a campaign group to fight the proposed development of the allotment site. Was she interested?

She certainly was. When she'd been walking along the towpath yesterday, she'd met Wilfred and Rita, and they'd been telling her the rumours about their allotments being sold for building were true. She'd pushed her concern aside while she'd been with Amy, but she had no intention of sitting quietly at home while others campaigned. She might be thinking of giving up her plot, but she didn't want to be forced into it.

She rang Bill back and said she'd do all she could to help. She could feel all her old energy returning as they discussed strategy, who to contact, and when to meet.

She wouldn't say anything to Mike or Amy yet. If they thought she still needed their combined efforts to keep her spirits up, she might be able to keep them in contact long enough for Mike to convince Amy he was serious about her, and could be trusted.

But was he? Had he gone to help Emma? Would the girl have wheedled her way back into his affections?

28

After breakfast on Sunday morning, Mike walked into San Sebastián and hired a car for the day. He'd eaten alone, Emma having opted to stay in her room, but when he spoke to her, she seemed calmer, though she was still refusing to report the loss of her bag to the authorities. She would not walk around town, in case she was seen by any of Eduardo's acquaintances, but agreed that being driven around the island would be better than staying in her hotel room all day.

He bought a map and a guidebook, and sat for a while at a pavement café, drinking coffee and watching people meeting up, chatting and passing the time of day.

He was amused to see the locals wearing jumpers and grumbling about the cold, while visitors like himself were ambling around in shorts and T-shirts.

The weather was warm and sunny, a complete contrast with the frost he'd left behind. If Amy were here they could have wandered around the town, watched the boats in the harbour, eaten at one of the many terraced cafés. If Amy were here, he'd be looking forward to the day's sightseeing, instead of filling in time until he could get Emma on a plane and home.

But she wasn't. She would have woken up to a cold winter's day in Hen Bont, probably cross because he'd let her down with no reasonable explanation. It was hard not to resent Emma. She should have phoned her parents, not dragged him into this mess.

He bought bottles of water, fruit and sandwiches, then drove back to the hotel and went up to her room.

'You'll have to navigate,' he said showing her the map. 'I thought we'd aim for the Garajonay National Park. There's a visitors' centre. Are you ready?'

'Almost. Where have you parked?'

'In the car park. Why?'

'Was there anyone in Reception?'

'There's no-one around. Come on, let's get out for a few hours.'

'You go. I'll come down in a few minutes. It's better no-one knows we're together.'

'Why not? And we're not together,' he said, regretting offering to take her with him. When she didn't reply, he shrugged and left her, determined to drive off alone if she didn't join him at the car park soon.

She scurried out five minutes later, looking nervously around, and jumped in the car quickly, keeping her head down, fiddling with the seatbelt fastening as he drove off.

He swallowed his irritation and handed her the map.

'Right. You'll have to direct me. The roads are supposed to be good, but precipitous. I'll need to concentrate on the driving.'

They navigated their way through San Sebastián onto the main road across the island, and Mike was relieved to see Emma was able to concentrate on something other than her troubles. As the car wound back and forward, up the twisting road out of the barranco, there was little time to admire the scenery, but there was a viewpoint once they reached the top, and she directed him to pull in there.

'I thought you might like to stop and look down at the harbour. Did you bring your camera?'

'Funnily enough, it wasn't top of my priorities when I packed,' he said dryly. 'I'll use my mobile.'

There was no hurry. It didn't matter if they never reached the visitors' centre. Mike was simply passing the time, and he knew Emma was desperate to be safe at home. Even so, the further they drove from San Sebastián, the more relaxed she became. They stopped at each mirador they came to, parking beside cars left by hikers who were following the walking trails, which disappeared down into the laurel forest. Signs pointed the way to villages far below. He longed to be following one of the routes, hand in hand with Amy. Instead, he was trying to make conversation with his ex.

Emma almost seemed to be enjoying herself as she read from the guidebook, telling him the history of the island, pointing out places they could see, almost as if they were on holiday. As if Eduardo had never happened and their life was as unruffled as it had been before.

Mike scowled, trying to ignore her voice as she read aloud. She had no idea what his trip to Gomera might have cost him. It was all about her. Had she even considered that he might have had something else to do rather than rush to her rescue?

She was calmly reading about some ancient legends as he took photos of the scenery to show Amy when he got home. He longed to bring her here. If she understood why he'd had to come, and forgave him.

'Princess Gara, of Gomera, fell in love with Jonay, a prince from Tenerife,' she read. 'Their parents disapproved and forbade them to meet, so they fled into the mountains. They were followed, so they climbed to the highest point of the island, and killed themselves. That's why the mountain peak is called Garajonay.

'Are you listening to me, Mike? Don't you think that's sad? Like Romeo and Juliet. Two people so in love they thought they couldn't live if they weren't together. I thought I loved Eduardo like that. I saw him and didn't care what anyone else thought. I'd have followed him anywhere.'

Mike came to sit beside her. 'Not quite anywhere,' he said. 'You weren't prepared to stay with him when you suspected he was involved in the drugs trade.'

'You must think I'm mad. Love at first sight! I left you and went chasing after a fantasy. It was a delusion. It all came crashing down at the first hint of trouble. I'm sorry.'

'If you hadn't fallen for Eduardo, you would have met someone else. We were together from habit. Love at first sight certainly isn't a fantasy.'

He sat on the sun-warmed rock, looking towards the spectacular Roque de Agando and down the valley towards Benchijigua, remembering a crispy autumn day on the aqueduct above the Dee Valley and his first meeting with Amy.

It had been love at first sight for him. That initial attraction had deepened in the following weeks, and he had been daring to hope her friendship would grow into love. Now that was all at risk. Would she believe his instinct to help Emma was loyalty to an old friend, or would she think he still had feelings for her? Aunt Meg certainly had her doubts. He needed to get home and start mending bridges.

Emma would have to call her parents. They could meet her at the airport and he could drive straight to Hen Bont without going back to Sheffield. He could be with Amy tomorrow evening.

Before he could speak Emma reached out her hand and tentatively took his.

'Mike. Tell me about her.'

'Who?'

'Whoever you've fallen in love with.'

He turned to look at her. She was curious, suddenly interested in what had happened to him since they'd parted, and determined to find out. He didn't want to talk about Amy. Not to her. He pulled his hand away and sat silently staring down into the pine forest, but she obviously wasn't going to give up. She knew him almost as well as his sister did.

'You just said love at first sight wasn't a fantasy,' she said. 'You always said it wasn't possible to love someone unless you knew them. Something must have happened to change your mind. Have you have met someone special? Come on, tell me.'

He laughed. Emma teasing and cajoling was better than having her terrified and crying over Eduardo.

He told her how he'd first met Amy, and how he'd thought he'd never see her again.

'Then Aunt Meg fell over and broke her arm. I went to see her and found

Amy had rented the cottage next door.'

'What a fantastic coincidence,' Emma said. 'So it's happy ever after?'

'Hardly,' Mike said. He told her how long it had taken him to persuade Amy he was someone worth spending time with.

'Maybe she'd been badly hurt by someone,' Emma said.

'I did wonder. We were going out for our first proper date this weekend.'

'So why the sighs and long face? It's wonderful, Mike. At least one of us should be happy.'

'She was at work when you rang me. I had to leave a message with Aunt Meg to tell her I wouldn't be turning up.'

'Because you came to help me.'

'Not your fault,' Mike said.

'If it's not my fault, whose is it? I've been so selfish. I never even considered that you might have more important things to do than rescuing me. I hope she understands when you explain.'

'I'm not sure she will. Aunt Meg doesn't. I told her I was going to help a

246

friend in trouble, but she guessed it was you.'

'She always did have a sixth sense.'

'She thought I was dropping everything because you called.'

'But you'd have done the same for your sister, or for a colleague in trouble. That's the sort of person you are, and I took advantage. I should have called my father.'

'Why didn't you?'

'I was afraid of what he would do. I thought he'd phone the police, and I didn't want that. I knew I could trust you.'

'I hope Amy thinks that she can trust me, when I get home.'

'Once you talk to her, she'll understand.'

'I wish I was as confident as you,' Mike said. 'You'll need to tell your parents everything, and quickly, because I'm going to have to tell Amy the whole story. Being evasive won't help. If you phone your father today, you could ask him to meet you at the airport. Then I could drive straight to Aunt Meg's and maybe see Amy tomorrow evening.'

Emma looked horrified. 'I can't,' she said. 'What would I say? I can't explain what's happened on the phone.'

'You could tell them you've had an argument with Eduardo and you're coming home.'

'What difference will another day make? You wouldn't be in Hen Bont until late in the evening.'

'I need to talk to Amy.'

'But straight off the plane? Before you've had time to rest? If you'll be staying with Aunt Meg for a while, won't you need a change of clothes? You'll want more than t-shirts and lightweight trousers. It's cold at home.'

Mike thought about it. His need to see Amy was overriding his common sense. It might be better to go home, repack his holdall, sleep, and drive across the next day.

'Maybe you're right,' he reluctantly agreed. 'But you must phone your parents as soon as we land. I'll drive you home and leave you to tell them what's been happening.'

He walked away, leaving her sitting on the rock, seemingly intent on watching a gecko that was foraging near her feet. He'd told Aunt Meg he hoped to be with her on Monday or Tuesday; now he knew it would be Tuesday morning, he should let her know.

He reached for his mobile and called her. There was no reply. He left a message. It was better this way. No need to go into lengthy explanations. Time enough for that later.

They drove back across the island towards town. Emma seemed happier, now that she knew they would soon be on the morning ferry on their way home, and didn't protest when he suggested they return the car, then walk up to the hotel together. As they walked, she pointed out the bench where she'd been sitting when her bag was stolen.

'I wasn't thinking straight,' she said. 'I left it on the bench while I stood looking out to sea. When I sat back down, it was gone.'

'Was anyone else around?'

'I was too preoccupied, wondering where Eduardo had sailed, to notice much. A few people were out walking. Sightseers, mostly.'

'Did you see which way they went?'

'Up the road, or along the footpath and through that gap in the wall, I suppose. Why?'

'Just a hunch,' Mike said. 'An opportunist thief would be after your money. They wouldn't want the handbag. I'm going to look.'

'I really want to get back to my room,' Emma said, looking about her anxiously.

'I won't be long,' he called over his shoulder, as he followed the path and began searching the undergrowth on the far side of the wall. 'What colour was your handbag?'

'Red. Why?'

'I think I've found it.'

She joined him as he reached into a patch of brambles trying to retrieve a bag, which had obviously been thrown away.

'That's it,' she said. 'And look, my wallet!'

He soon retrieved the handbag, though her wallet had fallen further into the undergrowth. There was no sign of her mobile phone, though as he stretched for the wallet, he saw a lipstick and hair-brush deep in the brambles, where they had obviously tumbled as the bag had been thrown. He ignored them and con-centrated on salvaging the wallet.

'Probably empty,' he said as he handed it to her.

It wasn't. The money was missing, but her credit cards were untouched. 'They just wanted the euros, and my mobile,' Emma said. 'The rest was no use to them. I feel so silly. I didn't think to look around. I just panicked. If I'd found this on Friday, I'd have been on the ferry Saturday morning, and home by now. I need never have bothered you.'

'As you said, you weren't thinking straight. You were already upset by Edu-ardo's behaviour, and losing your bag made everything more difficult. It's not surprising you panicked.'

'I overreacted,' she said. 'Maybe my misgivings about Eduardo were an overreaction as well. I didn't give him a chance to explain.'

'He had plenty of time to explain. He was being very secretive. It sounded far more than business confidentiality. I still think you should take your concerns to the police.'

'I've nothing to tell them, only vague suspicions. They won't be interested in the fact he left me stranded.'

29

Amy left for work early Monday morning, but as promised, called to see Meg before she went.

'Are you sure you'll be all right if I go straight from work for this meal?' she said. 'I can easily cancel it.'

'You go,' Meg insisted. 'I can cook meals for myself now, though I'm always glad of your company. I'm going to walk along to Pete's café and have a cup of tea with Madge and Emrys this afternoon. I expect Mike will phone once he's landed back in the UK.'

Amy would have welcomed an excuse not to go out with her colleagues. They all seemed very friendly, Sally in particular, but she hadn't been out with a group of friends since before she met Justin.

Meg was well able to look after herself, though. She would be having the strapping off her arm soon. After a few weeks, she should be back to normal, fit and healthy again in time for Christmas.

There was no plausible reason not to go; so, after her shift, she found herself being swept along with the others into an Italian restaurant. As the conversation ebbed and flowed around her, she was drawn into the friendly atmosphere. She'd forgotten the pleasure of casual conversation with no hidden agenda, of cheerful banter, the sharing of anecdotes and moans about the day's work. She'd cut herself off too long.

She had just ordered her food when Mike phoned. Excusing herself, she stepped outside to talk to him.

'I'm so sorry I had to cancel our dinner,' he said.

'No problem, Mike. It was only a meal, after all. Meg was disappointed you didn't come, but I took her out and kept her cheerful.'

'Our plane's just landed. I'll be coming over to Aunt Meg's tomorrow,' Mike said. 'I hope, when I explain what happened, you'll understand.'

'You don't have to explain yourself to me,' Amy said. 'But I'm glad you're back safely. Meg will be pleased to see you. I must go now. I'm out with friends, and I can see my meal has just arrived.'

'Will I see you tomorrow?'

'I'm on a twelve-hour shift, and I won't be leaving the hospital until eight o'clock, but I usually call in to see Meg before I go home. I'll see you briefly then.'

She switched her phone off and rejoined the group, reviewing the conversation in her mind. She was pleased with herself. She thought she had managed to imply their date had been of little importance, and that it was only his aunt who would be pleased to see him. No-one seemed to notice her preoccupation as they ate, talked about their latest partners, their plans for holidays, and the latest television drama.

The food was excellent, the company friendly, but she was relieved when she could eventually plead tiredness and go home.

Sally opted to leave as well. As they walked to the car park, she suggested Amy join them next time they all went out together.

'I'd like that,' Amy said. As she drove home, she reflected how much she had enjoyed the company, even though it had been impossible to keep Mike out of her thoughts. Which was the reason she had to be firm with herself and keep her distance.

She dared not risk loving again, and she was perilously close to loving Mike. What was there not to love? She'd been physically attracted to him from the moment they met, but over these past weeks she'd found he was kind, thoughtful and loyal. Even when he'd broken their date, it had been to help a friend. If that friend was Emma, and his explanation finished with him declaring that he was back with her, she had nothing to reproach him for.

It would be more difficult if he came home, having rescued Emma from some scrape from loyalty, not from love, and wanted to rearrange their date. It would be so hard not to give in, but the depth of her disappointment when he failed to turn up was ample warning that this could never be a casual friendship. She needed to keep as far away from him as she possibly could.

Her shift at the hospital next day was hectic, which had the advantage of blocking wayward thoughts about Mike from her mind. It was only as she left the building, and battled her way through the icy rain to her car, that she wondered if he'd arrived safely.

She might have decided to be cool and unconcerned when she saw him, but her body wasn't listening. She felt as if she were a seven-year-old at the top of the scenic railway at the seaside, her heart pounding with anticipation.

She turned on the radio. The rain might be bitterly cold, but the roads were clear, with no sign of ice. There had been weather warnings that morning for snow across the Pennines. It was a notoriously exposed route in severe weather, and Mike would have needed to drive that way. He might have seen the forecast and decided not to come.

In spite of everything, she yawned. She was very tired. She couldn't face Mike tonight. If he hadn't arrived, Meg would be disappointed, so she'd call in, have a friendly cup of tea, a quiet chat, and then go home to bed. If his car was there, she'd go straight home. She had another early shift next morning.

She turned into the courtyard, and all thoughts of a peaceful evening evaporated as she saw his car parked neatly outside Meg's. By the time she'd manoeuvred carefully into her own space, Meg's cottage door had opened and he stood framed in the doorway, the light spilling out around him.

She longed to be able to walk into his arms and welcome him home, to curl up beside him while he told her where he'd been, and why. The desire was overwhelming. She tried to convince herself it was just that she was tired, but knew it wasn't true. It was going to be so hard to listen, and pretend to be pleased for him, when he told her he was back with Emma.

She hesitated, wondering what to do. The sensible thing would be to put off talking to him until tomorrow, when she would finish work by early afternoon, be less tired, and more able to react rationally. If he was going straight back to Sheffield in the morning, she was sure Meg would tell her what had happened.

That would be the sensible decision. But he was already hurrying out to the car, holding Meg's huge black umbrella. All she needed to say was that she was tired, and would catch up with him later, but the words remained unsaid.

'Are you coming in, or are you going to sit in the car all night?' he said, opening the car door and smiling down at her.

All her sensible resolutions evaporated. She grinned. She couldn't help herself. It was so good to see him. She allowed herself to be ushered into Meg's cottage, sheltering under the brolly, savouring the warmth of his arm across her shoulders.

30

Mike had been anxiously peering out of the window, waiting for Amy, for the past half an hour.

'Standing there won't make her come any quicker,' Meg told him. 'She may be tired and go straight home when she sees your car.'

He came back into the room and perched on the arm of the settee.

'Because she doesn't want to talk to me?'

'Because she'll know I have company.'

She was late. He returned to the window. The rain, lashing against the glass, was on the verge of turning into snow.

'I hope she's safe. The roads were difficult when I drove here.'

'She's not driving over the Pennines, she's coming from Wrexham, and you checked the condition of the local roads ten minutes ago,' Meg said. 'Stop fretting. She's often late. She can't just walk off if she's dealing with a patient at the end of her shift.'

* * *

He'd been exhausted when he arrived at Hen Bont at lunchtime. Last night, Emma had phoned her parents from the airport, as she'd promised. He'd been concerned she'd try to delay and ask him to let her stay at his flat overnight, but he'd been determined to refuse. He'd done enough for her. Now it was time to get on with his own life.

While Emma was talking to her parents, he had phoned Amy. He wanted to hear her voice. He wanted to talk to her. But, far from reassuring him, the brief conversation had been disturbing. She was friendly, but casual and unconcerned. She was out with friends. That was good, wasn't it? He was pleased she was enjoying herself. But he'd expected her to be cross, or at least cool with him. She hadn't sounded cross, she'd sounded indifferent.

Would she understand why he had needed to go? How much could he tell her?

'I'm going to Aunt Meg's tomorrow. I'll have to tell her what happened,' he said to Emma as he drove along the motorway from the airport.

'Can't you say I had an argument with Eduardo? Tell her he left me stranded, then my handbag was stolen so I couldn't get home?'

'Aunt Meg has known you for years. She knows you're used to travelling abroad for your work. She'd guess there was more to it. What are you going to tell your parents?'

'I'm not sure. I'm worried about how Dad will react if he knows the whole story. He'll be so angry. He may try to contact Eduardo's family.'

'But your parents are not going to believe it was just an argument that panicked you into phoning me any more than Aunt Meg will.'

'Please don't say anything about my

suspicions, not yet.'

'And if Aunt Meg thinks you realised you'd made a mistake going off with Eduardo, and took the opportunity to play the damsel in distress?'

'I'm not like that,' Emma said. 'Aunt Meg knows I'm not like that.'

'Aunt Meg didn't think you'd give up everything to sail into the sunset with a man you hardly knew. She may well think you were overemphasising the situation you found yourself in.'

'Did you think that?'

'No. I could hear the panic in your voice. And I know any romance between us is long dead. Others don't. And what am I going to tell Amy? She needs to know I had reason to be genuinely worried about you.'

'I forgot about Amy,' Emma said.

Mike was furious. He concentrated on his driving, his hands gripping the wheel, his face rigid. It was typical of Emma, thinking only of herself. Yesterday, when he'd told her about Amy, she had been sympathetic, and apologised for not even thinking he may have arrangements to change in order to rush to help her. But that had all been forgotten now she faced the upcoming confrontation with her worried parents.

He didn't speak again until they were driving through the outskirts of Sheffield.

'I won't see Amy until tomorrow,' he said. 'That will give you plenty of time to tell your parents everything.'

She didn't reply. Mike pulled into a lay-by and turned to her.

'What you decide to do is up to you,' he said. 'But I am going to tell Amy the whole story. If she'll listen.'

'She'd be mad not to,' Emma said quietly. 'You're right. I was being thoughtless. And you've done so much for me. I had no right to ask you, but I am grateful.'

Mike put the car back into gear and pulled back into the traffic.

'Do you think you could ask Aunt Meg not to mention my suspicions about the drugs to your mother, or Lynda? I'll ask Mum and Dad not to talk about it, either. Now I'm back home it all seems so silly.'

'I doubt anyone will be interested after a few days,' Mike said. 'I'll tell Aunt Meg you think the fewer people who know, the better. She'll probably agree with you.'

'Thank you,' Emma said, as they turned into her driveway and her parents came rushing out to hug her.

He firmly refused their invitation to come in, saying Emma would fill them in with the whole story, but her father lingered by the car as Emma disappeared indoors with her mother.

'Whatever she's been up to, I'm sure we've cause to be grateful to you,' he said.

Mike assured him Emma would explain, said he was glad she was safe at home, and left as soon as he could. He'd always liked Emma's parents, but now was not the time to chat. They needed to talk to their daughter and he needed to sleep.

He was exhausted, but sleep didn't

265

come easily, and when it did his dreams were disjointed and bizarre. Emma would be sharing her experiences with her parents, while he was forced to wait until the following day before he could talk to Aunt Meg, and until the evening before he could see Amy.

He drove to Hen Bont in the morning, arriving in time for lunch. Aunt Meg listened as he told her the whole story, from Emma's first phone call, to her request for Meg not to talk about her suspicions about Eduardo. Then he'd told her how he'd phoned Amy from the airport, and now wished he hadn't.

She let him talk, asking the occasional question, but not giving an opinion, until he mentioned Amy.

'I'm not surprised she seemed distant,' she said. 'You persuaded her to go for a meal with you, then you left a message to say you couldn't make it. It didn't take her long to deduce you'd gone to help a former girlfriend. Did you expect her to be pleased?'

'No, but once I explain ... '

266

He stopped when he saw the doubtful look on his aunt's face.

'You'll need to give her a good explanation.'

'But if I tell her what I told you … '

'That your former girlfriend was in trouble and you ran to help her?'

Put like that, it sounded so much worse than it was. He longed to be able to hold Amy close, kiss her and tell her the truth, that once they'd met on the aqueduct no-one else would ever come close to his feelings for her. But apart from fleeting moments, which could have been wishful thinking, Amy had given him no sign she felt the same way. She was beginning to like his company, certainly, but was that all? He sensed that if he spoke too soon she would withdraw and return to being cautiously friendly.

At last he saw the lights of her car turning into the courtyard. He opened the door and stood watching as she parked, then could wait no longer and ran out to meet her. She smiled as he opened the car door. It was so good to see her. He could barely stop himself from hugging her as she got out of the car. He hurried her into the cottage, his arm around her shoulders. It was going to be all right.

His optimism was soon dashed. He had to keep reminding himself that he'd seen the smile of welcome on her face before she ducked her head under the umbrella. For that instant, he had been certain she was as pleased to see him as he was to see her. It had felt right. Welcoming her home. He wanted to be there when she came in from work every night.

But, as he furled the umbrella and turned to take her coat, the atmosphere changed.

'I won't stay,' she said briskly. 'I need to get home. It's been a long day.'

'Won't you have a cup of tea with us?' Meg asked.

'No thank you, not this evening. I'm glad you're home safely, Mike. Are you going back to Sheffield tomorrow?'

'No. I'm staying at least for the rest of the week. Can we talk soon? Maybe rearrange our dinner? I'm so sorry I had to cancel. I need to explain why.'

'No need to explain to me,' she said. 'It's not as if it was a date. You were just taking me out to thank me for looking after Meg. You didn't need to. Meg and I are friends, aren't we, Meg? I don't need thanks.'

Then she had left.

31

Meg watched the interplay between Amy and Mike. Saw their faces alive with joy as they came indoors, only for the light to go out of Amy's eyes and the mask to come down.

Mike's smile had wavered, faded, then changed to a frown as Amy made her excuses and left. The whole incident lasted less than five minutes. If it wasn't for the dripping wet umbrella, and the miserable look on Mike's face, she could have imagined they were still waiting for Amy to come home from work.

'You'll be able to talk to her tomorrow,' she said. 'She's only working in the morning.'

Mike slumped onto the settee, tiredness etched on his face. But he looked far too tense to sleep.

'I don't think she wants to see me,' he said.

'She was tired. She's often tired after a long shift.'

'She did seem pleased when I went out to the car … ' His voice trailed away.

'I think I'll go out for a run before I go to bed,' he said, after a while spent pacing around the room. 'Do you mind?'

'Not at all, but it's still raining.'

'When has a bit of rain ever stopped me going out? Or you either?' he teased. 'I've brought my wet-weather gear, and there's a torch in the car. Are you coming with me?'

She laughed as she saw his mood change. A run would do him good. While he was gone, she sat by the fire, thinking about Amy. It was true that she often came home drained after a difficult day, but she'd always said how much she appreciated the chance to have a chat and unwind quietly, before going back to her empty cottage. Had she meant it? Or was she simply being kind? Now, with Mike dropping in frequently, Amy might feel she could step back.

Or had she left so swiftly to avoid

spending time with Mike? Was she cross with him for breaking their date? She might not want to get involved with someone who was still rushing around after an ex-girlfriend. He might have a cool reception tomorrow.

* * *

Next morning, Mike insisted on making Meg breakfast, before taking her shopping so that she could stock her food cupboards. They chatted about Christmas, and how pleased Gwen was she'd agreed to stay until after the New Year, but Meg could see he was preoccupied; and, a short while after Amy returned from work, he went to see to her.

He'd only just left when Bill rang to report progress on the campaign to save the allotments.

'We need to set up our first committee meeting,' he said. 'There's you, me, Wilfred, Rita, Alicia and Fred. He says it won't do any good, but he'll help where he can.'

Meg laughed. 'That sounds like Fred. Where and when?'

'Alicia says we can meet in her house if we want to. It'll be easier for her, with the children. We were thinking Friday afternoon.'

Meg agreed, and they spent a while discussing tactics and who they should contact. She felt more energised than she had since her fall, and was eager to tell Mike about their plans. However, when he returned from seeing Amy, it was obvious from the distressed look on his face that their talk had not gone well.

'Did she not understand?' she asked, cautiously.

'She understood,' he said. 'She said I did right to go and help Emma. She said she could see why I hadn't been able to phone her myself. She said she had thought I would phone her when I arrived, wherever I was going, but after all I had only been taking her out to thank her for helping you after your accident. She said we both understood that. She reminded me she didn't need thanks, she likes your company, and enjoys help-ing you.'

'That's good, then, isn't it?' Meg said.

'Good? What's good about it? She accepts I only helped Emma out of friendship, but she didn't seem to think it was any of her business whether I wanted to get back with Emma or not. She was so distant. Like she was after we first met. She's shut me out, Aunt Meg. I asked her if she'd like to come for a walk this afternoon, but she declined. Very politely, but she still said no.'

'Did she say she had to wash her hair?' Meg said, trying to lighten the mood.

'Not quite.' Mike half-smiled. 'She said she had to wash her clothes. Would you like to go for a stroll, Aunt Meg?'

'I'm going to turn you down too. I think you need a long run, not a quiet walk. I'm going to read a book, then you can cook me dinner.'

When Mike had left for his run, Meg thought about going to see Amy, but decided to leave her to her washing. She and Mike were so obviously attracted to each other, it would be a pity if Emma's escapade ruined things for them, but they would have to sort things out themselves. There was little she could do to help, except maybe try to keep them in contact, which was difficult now that she didn't really need their assistance.

★ ★ ★

Over the next few weeks Mike, visited Meg frequently. He was there to take her for her final visit to the clinic, and to encourage her when she found difficulty getting the strength back in her arm. He spent time looking for somewhere to rent near Betteley Locks, and said he planned to move after Christmas, ready to start his job in the New Year.

On one of his visits, he told Meg he'd seen Emma. Eduardo's parents had contacted her to say he'd been arrested in South America. It was fortunate he'd left her on La Gomera, or she might have been arrested, too. She'd had nothing to do with anything illegal, but it might have been difficult to explain that.

'Do you ever think of going back to Emma?' Meg asked.

'Never. We'll probably stay friends, but that's all either of us wants. She starts a new job soon, and is putting her life back in order. I'll be working on my new project in January.'

'And Amy?'

'Amy is making it clear she wants no more than a casual friendship. It's not what I want, but I'm going to have to accept it.'

When he and Amy met, Meg saw that she was polite, friendly even, but the animated, cheerful girl she knew was guarded in his company. She tried to include her in any walks they planned, and asked her to accompany them when they ate out, but Amy was always busy doing something else. Yet when Mike wasn't there she was as friendly as ever, dropping in frequently, as she had before.

It was obvious they were both unhappy, but it became increasingly difficult to even keep them in the same room. Meg wondered if Amy had been badly hurt in the past, but unless she confided in her there was nothing she could do.

She had been warned it would be a while before she regained the full use of her arm, but she was determined to be back to full strength by the time she went to Gwen's for the Christmas holiday. She intended to spend time with Lily, and to give Gwen a rest, not to be another person for her to look after.

The campaign to save the allotments was gaining momentum. Meg told Amy about it when she came in one evening and found half the committee discussing their next moves. Amy had been enthusiastic.

'Does Mike know about this?' she asked.

Meg admitted he didn't.

'You'll have to tell him. He could help you when he comes to visit. Remember when we first met, and you didn't want him to know about the allotment?'

Meg laughed and agreed to tell him. Once Christmas was over it would be impossible to convince Mike she still needed his help. He would still visit when he started his new job, but not nearly as often. It was a pity. Especially as it seemed Amy might be thawing a little towards him. It was the first time in weeks she had willingly brought his name into the conversation.

He had agreed he would come to fetch her a few days before Christmas. She'd arranged for a meeting of the allotment committee at her cottage the day before he was expected. Everyone was there, arguing about the best way forward. Meg was all for taking some sort of dramatic action to highlight the campaign.

'I think we should blockade the road,' she said. 'If we all have placards, and invite the news reporters, they'll have to take notice.'

That was when Mike came in.

'Placards, protest meetings – what's going on, Aunt Meg?'

She filled him in on the details, and he was soon joining in the conversation, making useful suggestions, and offering to help where he could. But once everyone had gone home he was irritated.

'You've been trying to fool me, Aunt Meg. Pretending you still needed my help.'

'Not really,' she said. 'I thought...'

'You were trying to keep me visiting so I'd see Amy. It won't work. I'll visit because I'll be living nearer, and I like your company, but I've given up any hope of Amy and I getting together. She's not interested.'

* * *

They left for Sheffield next day. As Mike loaded the car, Amy came out to say goodbye. Meg hugged her, before settling into the passenger seat. She heard Amy wishing Mike a happy Christmas. Was it her imagination, or did the girl's voice sound wistful, full of regrets? She didn't hear Mike's reply. Someone was trying to drive a red Ferrari into the courtyard, sounding the horn loudly when he saw there was no space.

Meg climbed back out of the car as

Amy retreated to her front door and Mike strode across to speak to the driver. After a short conversation, she heard his raised voice.

'You'll have to reverse. Drive round the block. I'll have gone by the time you get back.'

As the car reversed, Mike called across to Amy that her friend would be back in a few minutes. Meg could hear the coldness in his voice, and could see from the stricken look on Amy's face that she had heard it, too. Or was she upset by the arrival of her visitor?

She would have gone to speak to her, but Mike was already fastening his seatbelt, and turning on the ignition.

'Come along, Aunt Meg. We need to go before that arrogant idiot returns.'

She returned to her seat and closed the door as he drove away, his face impassive, his eyes angry.

'He said he'd come to see to Amy Weston,' he said bitterly. 'She's welcome to him. Why didn't she say she had a boyfriend?'

32

Amy was horrified when she saw Justin attempting to enter the courtyard. She scurried back to her cottage, sick with apprehension, as Mike went to speak to him. Her fears increased as Justin reversed out, and Mike jumped into his car and drove away, after calling out that her 'friend' would be back in a few minutes. The word 'friend' had been almost shouted, Mike's voice heavy with sarcasm. What had Justin said to cause him to react with such disdain?

The cottages suddenly felt very isolated. She ran inside, slammed the door, then bolted it, trembling as much from distress at the chill in Mike's voice as from her fear of Justin. She should have confided in him weeks ago, when he'd returned from La Gomera and told her why he'd gone to help Emma. It would have been the ideal moment to explain why she could never be more than casual friends with anyone.

It was too late now. It had only been Meg's increasingly contrived meetings between the three of them that had kept the tenuous friendship alive. Now Mike had driven off with such a look of contempt on his face, she thought he was unlikely to want to contact her again.

How had Justin had found out where she lived? She leaned back against the door, cowering inside her own cottage. Had he seen her? Could she pretend to be out?

It was only a short time before she heard his car negotiating the narrow entrance into the courtyard. He parked in the only space available, where Mike's car had been standing only a few moments before.

Why was she hiding? A surge of anger swept through her. He no longer had any power to hurt her. It was time to tell him so.

She unbolted the door and opened it just before he knocked. He stood, one hand raised to hammer at the door, the other clutching a bouquet of red roses. A sudden sleety squall drenched him as he stepped forward, hastily rearranging his face into a smile.

This was the man she'd been frightened of for so long? It was time to finish it.

'Justin! What do you want?' She stood in the doorway, seemingly impervious to the cold, blocking his entry.

'Are you going to invite me in? I'm getting soaked,' he said, thrusting the flowers at her.

'I think not,' she said.

He looked confused, then irritated, as once again he pushed the flowers towards her, and once again she ignored them.

'But I need to talk to you. I've missed you,' he pleaded.

'Really?' she said, coolly. 'Actually, there are a few things I need to say to you, too.'

'So, let me in and we'll talk.'

His lips were smiling, but the smile didn't reach his eyes. How had she ever found him attractive?

'Drive out of here and park in the car park in the High Street,' she said. 'Pay for half an hour. It won't take longer than that. Go into the café. I'll meet you there in a few minutes.'

She closed the door as he began to object, ignored his repeated knocking and protestations, and waited until he'd driven away before she moved.

She was no longer frightened of him. The first shock of his arrival had worn off. He had looked pathetic as he stood on her doorstep, dripping wet, with his bunch of hothouse roses clutched in his hand. He seemed unable to believe she hadn't thrown herself into his arms with a glad cry of joy.

Again, she wondered how he had found where she lived. She needed to find out, then she would tell him exactly what she thought of him, and what she would do if he ever tried to contact her again.

Before walking along the road to the café she parked her own car in the entrance to the courtyard so that no-one could drive in. When she'd said all she intended to, she thought it unlikely Justin would attempt to follow her back, but with the next-door cottage empty, it was best to be cautious.

He was standing outside the café, this time holding an umbrella. She wondered fleetingly what he'd done with the flowers. Would he recycle them? Offer them to his latest conquest?

'Amy, this is silly. We can't talk in a crowded café,' he blustered, but she pushed past him and went inside. After a few moments, he folded his umbrella and followed her.

'Hello, Amy. Usual?' Pete called out.

'Yes please,' she said, as she headed for the table in the window. 'And a mug of tea.'

'I don't like tea,' Justin grumbled as he sat opposite her. 'Surely you remember that?'

Amy smiled sweetly. She remembered only too well. He didn't like his drinks in mugs, either. And he certainly wouldn't like the cosy, friendly atmosphere in this cheerful café, where she knew every one of the customers.

'Forget the tea, Pete,' Amy called. 'My former acquaintance won't be staying long.'

Pete came across with a mug of steaming hot chocolate for her.

'Let me know if there's anything else you need,' he said, casting a dubious glance at Justin.

Amy relaxed as Pete returned to the counter. Justin wouldn't dare try to bluster and bully her here.

'Right,' she said, stirring her drink. 'How did you find out where I lived?'

'Let me explain first,' he said. 'I understand why you're being so cold to me, after we parted so acrimoniously.'

'You mean, after I found out you were married with young children, and I told you I never wanted to see you again? After you threatened to end my career if your wife ever found out about me? After you...'

She spoke quietly, so no-one else

286

could hear, but Justin looked around him, increasingly uncomfortable.

'I'm sure I didn't say half those things. I would never do anything to hurt you. Surely you know that? I was devastated when you left. I didn't want to lose you.'

'Or your wife and children,' she said.

'She's left me. We're getting divorced. There's no reason why we can't be together now. I know that's what you want.'

His confidence was returning. She could see that, even now, he thought she would welcome him back.

She stared at his smooth, self-assured smile, and wondered how she could ever have believed herself in love with him.

'You think I would want to be with someone who cheats on his wife and young children? Who uses threats to try to get his own way? I wouldn't trust you not to lie about anything if it suited you.'

He reached over the table and attempted to take her hand. She snatched it away from him and picked up her mug of hot chocolate, forcing herself to sip at it, while she glared at him over the rim.

'Your mother thinks you still love me,' he said. 'She told me when I rang her and said I wanted to get in touch with you.'

Amy's hand shook. She placed her mug carefully back on the table.

'You rang my mother?' she whispered.

'I did,' he smirked, obviously delighted to be getting a reaction at last. 'I told her I bitterly regretted the way we'd parted, and I wanted to talk to you, to apologise if I'd done anything to upset you.'

It was almost impossible not to shriek at him, but she managed to control her voice and speak quietly.

'Did you tell her I'd found out you were married?'

'Of course not. It was obvious from her reaction that you hadn't said anything...'

'I was too ashamed,' Amy said. 'And you'd threatened me.'

He laughed. 'I was desperate that you shouldn't tell my wife,' he said. 'I wouldn't have actually done anything.

288

Surely you knew that? But she found out anyway, a short while after you'd left me.'

Amy decided it was time to finish the conversation.

'She'd known for ages,' Amy said. 'She knew about the other affairs, too. Did you never stop to ask yourself how I had found out? Your wife told me. I promised her I wouldn't tell you. She needed time to plan her life without you.'

Now she had rattled him. She watched the conflicting emotions rush across his face, then looked at her watch.

'Right, it's time for you to go. You don't want to get a parking ticket. I don't want to hear from you again. Ever. Understand?'

He stood, towering over her, but he no longer had the power to disturb her.

'But I love you ... ' he stuttered.

'You don't know what love is,' she sighed.

'Did you want another drink, Amy?' Pete asked as he came across to their table.

'Actually, I'll order lunch,' she said.

'My visitor is just leaving.'

Pete made no move to return to the counter, but started to describe the items on the specials board in great detail until Justin gave up and left. She watched him stride across the road and into the car park, and a few minutes later saw his car being driven away, far faster than safety, or the speed limit, allowed.

'Hope he doesn't knock anyone over,' Pete murmured. 'Did you really want lunch, or was that just a ploy to get rid of him?'

'Thanks, Pete.' She grinned. 'I will have lunch. I'm suddenly very hungry.'

33

Amy returned to her cottage after her lunch, light-headed with relief. Her fear of confronting Justin again had been affecting her decisions ever since their acrimonious break-up. She'd been worried about how she would react if they met; now she knew. He no longer frightened or disturbed her in any way. It was over.

She wasn't concerned that he would continue to pursue her. He'd come to her because he wanted someone to tell him how wonderful he was, to boost his ego until he was able to convince himself it was his decision to break his marriage. Now he knew she wasn't interested, he wouldn't be back.

She pushed past her car, still blocking the entrance to the courtyard, and decided to leave it there. She needed to rest for a few hours before she left for work. The first day back on nights was always difficult, but she surprised herself by sleeping. Three nights' work, then she'd be going to stay with her parents for a few days.

It was the first Christmas she'd been able to spend at home for years. She had been looking forward to it, but her anger at her mother was threatening to spoil the holiday.

Why had she given Justin her address? It seemed uncharacteristically irresponsible. Obviously nothing she had said over the past months had convinced her mother she was no longer in love with him. How much of that was her own fault? Her mother could see she was still distressed, and assumed Justin had broken the relationship. She shouldn't have let her go on thinking he'd left her. She'd been too ashamed to admit the truth.

Meg phoned to say they'd arrived safely.

'The roads were clear, but there was a lot of snow across the Pennines,' she said. 'It was a beautiful drive. You take care when you go home. I won't keep you. You'll be off to work soon. Have a lovely Christmas with your parents.'

'Say Happy Christmas to Mike for me,' Amy said.

'You should phone him yourself,' Meg said, before ringing off.

Amy sat holding the phone. After the way Mike had looked at her before he left there was no way she could phone him. Was Meg cross with her, too?

She had sounded a bit abrupt. She must be wondering who it was who'd come to see her, and why she hadn't mentioned she was expecting someone. What must Mike have thought? Had he seen those flowers? Hard to see how he could have missed them.

Justin was out of her life. She would tell her parents what had happened, but she'd left it too late to explain to Mike. She prepared for work, grateful that her job was totally absorbing. There wouldn't be time to fret while she was there.

It was very quiet in the cottage with Meg away. Amy missed her company, but most of all she missed Mike. Over the past weeks, if he hadn't actually been next door, he'd been expected soon. He'd always been in her thoughts. She'd struggled not to watch for his car, not to be delighted when she saw him. She'd done a good job of hiding how she felt.

She'd thought he'd accepted it. The last few times she'd seen him, their conversations had been as casual as her banter with other people she met occasionally. But the look he'd given her, as he'd said her 'friend' would be back in a few minutes, said otherwise. A casual friend wouldn't have minded. And he had minded. Hurt, anger, and bewilderment had chased across his face, followed by a contemptuous shrug, as he got in his car and drove off. He must have thought she'd been keeping him at arm's length because she already had a boyfriend. A boyfriend she'd forgotten to mention.

If he had still been attracted to her, Justin's arrival had killed that attraction. Wasn't that what she wanted? Hadn't she spent the last few months trying to

convince him she wanted only friendship? But that was because she'd been
allowing Justin to influence her life, even
though they'd parted. Why should she
make herself miserable, rejecting any
possibility of happiness, because of the
duplicity of one man?

If only she could go back to the via-
duct and her first encounter with Mike,
and start again. But she'd left it too late.

She was relieved when she finished
her last shift and set off to the Lake District for Christmas. Her parents were
delighted to see her. They had talked
about visiting the cottage, but she'd put
them off until she was settled, then they'd
been to visit her sister in Canada, and
since then there hadn't been a mutually
convenient time.

'We must visit early in the New Year,'
her mother said, once Amy had carried
her cases in and they were settled around
a huge log fire.

'That would be great, Mum. But
there's something I need to tell you
before you come.'

'It's about Justin, isn't it?' her mother interrupted. 'You're back together. He came to see us. He was so apologetic about not being in touch, but he obviously didn't want to make us feel uncomfortable.'

Amy jumped to her feet. 'We are not back together. What's he been saying? And what possessed you to give him my address?'

'There's no need to talk to your mother like that,' her father said. 'We gave him your address so he could contact you. He obviously thinks a lot of you and missed you dreadfully.'

Amy had been intending to wait until after Christmas to have this conversation, but there was no point in waiting any longer. Her parents were both looking at her, confused and upset.

'Why don't you pour us all a drink, Dad?' she said, as she sat back down. 'It's time I told you what happened. I know you've been worried about me, but I was too upset to tell anyone.'

'Not even us?' her father said, handing her a glass of wine.

'Especially you and Mum. I was so ashamed.'

'Ashamed because you'd fallen out with Justin?' her mother said. 'Why? All couples have arguments.'

'It was far more than an argument,' Amy said. 'But at last I can see that it wasn't my fault.'

'What wasn't?' her mother said.

'I thought I loved him,' she began. 'He worked long hours, and I was working shifts, but when we did meet it was magical. No-one else at the hospital knew we were together. Justin didn't want others talking about what only concerned us. We wouldn't see each other, except in passing at work, then he'd arrive with his arms full of flowers, and whisk me away for a romantic break at a country hotel.'

'Like the time he booked that weekend in Kendal and you brought him to meet us?' her mother said.

'Yes, but his reaction to finding out you lived so near should have alerted me that something was wrong. When I told him, he was so upset he wanted to leave. But he was important to me, I wanted you to meet him, and this seemed a perfect time. He eventually agreed to come, though he was cross and hardly spoke to me on the short drive over.'

'But he was charming to us,' Mum said. 'He didn't seem in the least annoyed.'

'He could turn on the charm when he needed to. Months later, I found out just why he wanted to keep our relationship a secret between the two of us when I had a phone call from his wife.'

34

'His wife?' Amy's father began pacing the room. He looked very angry.

'Sit down, dear. You're making the girl nervous,' her mother said. 'Or, better still, refill our glasses.'

Her mother reached out her hand and took one of Amy's, while her father picked up the bottle of wine and topped up their drinks.

Amy took a sip, and then continued. 'His wife told me she'd found my number on his mobile phone. She'd been checking up on him. It wasn't the first time he'd had an affair. She said he got fed up of coming home to a house full of babies and children.'

'He was married! With children!' Her mother was horrified.

'Three. All under five. His wife sounded so tired and defeated. I was devastated for her. I'd been so easily deceived. I knew I could never trust anyone again. She said it might not be his first affair, but it would be the last time he'd be unfaithful. She was leaving him. When I confronted him, he didn't deny his family. How could he? But he threatened to make my life a misery if his wife ever found out. I didn't tell him she was the person who'd alerted me. She'd asked me not to. She wanted time to make her plans. I applied for a post at another hospital, moved to a new town and started again.'

'Telling no-one, not even us,' her mother said.

'I was so ashamed. I felt so guilty.'

'What had you got to feel guilty about? He's a deceitful, cheating rat,' her father said. He was trembling with anger. Amy remembered how he had defended both her and her sister when they fell out with friends, or got into mischief at school. Her mother reached out and patted his arm.

'Calm down, love,' she said. 'You getting worked up isn't going to help. I'm so sorry, Amy. We had no idea. We thought he'd left you and that was why you were so upset.'

Amy remembered the numerous phone calls, the anxious enquiries about new friends.

'How could you have known, Mum? I didn't want you to know. I didn't want anyone to know.'

'But you'd done nothing wrong,' her father said. 'And he had the cheek to phone us and ask how you were.'

'I answered the phone,' her mother said. 'He was very hesitant. Wondered if you were staying with us. I said you weren't here, but offered to pass on a message; then he asked if he could call in to see us. He said he was in the area.'

'There didn't seem any reason to say no,' her father added. 'He had a cup of coffee, said how much he missed you, that he regretted the way you had split up, and he wanted to talk to you. He had us completely fooled. What did he really want with you?'

'His wife is divorcing him. He thought

I'd fall into his arms and forgive him. I suppose he wanted to be able to say he was leaving her because he'd fallen in love with someone else. How they were both going to move on with their lives, and the children wouldn't suffer. Sounds better than admitting she threw him out, after a string of affairs. Justin always cared about appearances. He wouldn't want people to think badly of him.'

'Can you ever forgive us?' her mother said, her eyes full of tears.

Amy hugged both her parents.

'It seems easier to accept, knowing he fooled you as well. I've been finding it difficult to trust anyone. He made me mistrust my judgement.'

'Most people are genuine,' her father said. 'That's why it's such a shock when you meet such a total...'

'Don't let the swine win by spending your life suspecting everyone,' her mother interrupted.

Amy burst out laughing. Her parents never swore – not in front of their children, anyway. But her father had certainly been about to, and her mother calling Justin a swine had replaced her mental picture of him with an image of a pig in a suit. She laughed until she cried. Cried, as she hadn't done since Justin's soon-to-be-ex-wife had phoned and shattered her illusions about him.

'Feel better now?' her mother asked, when she finally stopped.

Amy nodded.

'Then let's enjoy Christmas. You can tell us all about life in your village and about your new friends. How's Meg's arm? Is it healed now?'

The few days break passed far too quickly. Amy told her parents about Meg, and kept them amused with stories about the old lady's exploits. Inevitably, Mike's name cropped up frequently.

'So is Mike just a friend?' her mother asked. 'Or is there something else you're not telling us?'

'There's nothing else.'

'But you'd like there to be,' her mother said. It wasn't a question. Amy was about to deny it, but there had been enough misleading and half-truths. If she'd confided in them sooner, they would never have told Justin where she lived.

'I do like Mike. I think he was attracted to me, too,' she said.

'Was?'

'I messed things up,' she admitted.

'Because of Justin?'

'I didn't want to get close to anyone else. I didn't want to be hurt again.'

'But you can't let that man ruin the rest of your life.'

'I know that now. But it's too late. I've pushed him away for weeks. Then he saw Justin arrive. He'll think...'

'He won't know what to think, unless you tell him the truth,' her mother said.

★ ★ ★

Amy returned to Hen Bont, knowing it was too late to mend her relationship with Mike, but thinking she owed him an explanation. As soon as he brought Meg home, she decided, she'd go to tell them both the whole story. Meg would understand. Would Mike?

She made good time. The thaw had set in and the roads were wet rather than icy. Her cottage was cold and unwelcoming. She kept her coat and scarf on as she unloaded the car, and dropped all her bags and boxes on the settee before turning up the heating and going into the kitchen to put the kettle on.

She was starting a few weeks of night shifts and, knowing she would be back at work the following evening, her mother had sent her home with a meal ready to pop in the microwave, and enough food to last several days. She started putting things into the fridge, feeling thoroughly miserable. The contrast with the warmth of her family home was stark. She loved her cottage, but it was lonely without Meg next door, and when she thought of Meg she thought of Mike and remembered the chill in his voice as he left.

She'd promised to check on Meg's cottage, and went next door while she still had her coat on. The place felt even colder than her own. She scooped up a pile of cards and circulars from the mat and put them on the coffee table. The dull grey light of late December hardly penetrated the room. She switched on the light and looked around. Nothing seemed out of place, but as well as being cold the air was musty and damp. She went towards the kitchen, alarmed to find her feet squelching as she walked across a wet carpet.

As soon as she opened the kitchen door, she could see the red quarry tiles were awash, and water was seeping down the wall from the bathroom above. She looked under the sink for the stop-cock, hoping it was in the same place as her own. It was. She turned it off, then headed for the stairs, reaching for her mobile as she went.

She didn't want to disturb Meg's holiday, but she needed to call a plumber, and it wasn't her house. She rang Mike, but his phone clicked through to message.

'Mike. Can you phone me, please? It's urgent,' she said.

If he didn't ring back, she'd have to ring Meg, but she wanted to speak to him first. It would be better if he could tell his aunt about the damage to her home.

The bathroom was in a worse state than the kitchen, and she could see water dripping through the ceiling. A pipe must have burst in the attic. She went back downstairs, wondering if the electricity was safe. She'd put the light on when she'd first come in, and the water didn't seem to be near the switches, but it was better to be cautious.

Mike still hadn't called her back. Maybe he would ignore her message. She couldn't wait much longer before calling Meg and ruining her holiday. She went home to fetch her torch, and just as she returned, he rang.

35

Mike was visiting his grandmother and Aunt Meg when Amy phoned. He saw her name on the display, but ignored it. He'd spent the whole holiday trying to convince himself he didn't mind about the suave stranger who'd turned up to see her. He hadn't missed the expensive red roses on the passenger seat of the Ferrari. There was probably a box of handmade chocolates done up in cellophane and red ribbon somewhere, too.

He'd been devastated. It wasn't Amy's fault he'd fallen in love with her, but she must have known how he felt. Why hadn't she told him she had a boyfriend? He would have respected that. But while he'd been helping Emma, worrying about how she would feel about him rushing to rescue his ex, Amy had been waiting for her current boyfriend to return.

He must have been away, probably

doing some business deal. Mike had taken an instant dislike to the man, knowing instinctively that he wouldn't make her happy. He'd be unlikely to enjoy helping her garden, or spend a day scrambling up steep mountain paths.

Why had she been so secretive? Even if she thought her friendship with him wasn't important, it was strange that she hadn't even mentioned him to Aunt Meg. She'd been as surprised as him. Hurt, too, he thought.

Annoyed as he was, that didn't stop his heart from beating faster at the thought of hearing her voice, but he wasn't going to listen to her message with his mother, grandmother and Aunt Meg all in the room, watching him.

Making an excuse that he needed something from the car, he pulled on his coat and went outside. He'd listen, but had no intension of calling her back.

'Mike. Can you phone me, please? It's urgent.'

Her voice was calm and measured, but there was no doubt she needed his help, and no doubt in his mind he would give it. As he phoned her, he knew he'd do anything for her.

'Mike. We've got a problem.'

He listened as she explained. In spite of what she was saying, and his concern about breaking the news to his aunt, it was good to hear from her.

'I'm with Mum and Aunt Meg now,' he said. 'I'll tell them, and then drive straight over. Aunt Meg probably knows a plumber. If they can come before I get there, could you let them in? Or are you going to work?'

'I'll be here. I've only just got back from the Lake District.'

'I'll phone you as soon as I've spoken to Aunt Meg. And Amy … thanks.'

* * *

Meg looked stricken when he told her about the burst pipes, but her practical nature soon took over.

'First things first,' she said, rif Iing in her handbag and producing her diary.

'I've got Henry's phone number here somewhere. Here we are.'

'Who's Henry?'

'A friend. He's a plumber. He still does some work, though his son runs the business.'

She rang Henry's mobile. He was already on an emergency call, but promised to go round to her cottage as soon as possible. She told him she was in Sheffield, then handed the phone over to Mike.

'I'll be there as soon as possible,' Mike said. 'But if you arrive before me, the lady who lives in the adjoining cottage has a key. She'll let you in.'

'I'll phone Amy, then go,' he told his aunt. 'I think it would be best if you stayed here.'

The kitchen sounded unusable, the bathroom was a mess, and the bedrooms might be damp. It would be easier if she stayed where she was while he sorted things out. He expected to have to try to dissuade her from coming with him, and looked to his mother for support. Surprisingly, he didn't need it.

'I agree,' Aunt Meg said. 'I'll only be in the way while the plumber does his work. You may need the electrician, too. I've got his number here.'

'You can stay with us as long as you like, you know that,' his mother said, as he went outside to phone Amy.

Before he closed the door he overheard his aunt's reply.

'Thanks, Gwen. I thought if he goes on his own it'll be a good chance for him and Amy to spend time together.'

Mike groaned. Spending time together wouldn't help. Aunt Meg needed to accept that any hopes he'd had of a future with Amy were over as soon as the obnoxious boyfriend turned up.

He had to accept it, too. He needed to be businesslike. He'd tell her he was on his way and ask her to open the cottage for the plumber if he arrived first. He wouldn't try to draw her into conversation by asking how she was, or if she'd enjoyed her Christmas break. Cool and efficient. That was the only way to cope.

He told her he was leaving soon and hoped to be with her before the plumber arrived.

'Last time you said you were leaving Sheffield soon, you went on a jaunt to the Canary Islands instead,' she said, disarming him with the unexpected teasing note in her voice.

He was smiling as he replied. 'I won't answer if anyone else rings. I can only cope with one crisis at a time.'

'Is Meg coming with you?'

'No, she's staying here. I'll be on my own.'

'See you later, then,' she said, and hung up, leaving him cradling the phone, wondering if he had imagined the warmth in her voice.

36

Once she knew Mike was on his way, Amy went back to her cottage and started unpacking her things. There was nothing more she could do until the plumber arrived.

She phoned her parents to say she was safely home and tell them what had happened. Her mother was predictably upbeat about Mike's imminent arrival.

'Tell him everything,' she advised. 'You've got nothing to lose.'

'He may not want to talk to me.'

'He won't if he thinks Justin is still in your life. Did you say Meg's kitchen was unusable? That meal I gave you for your supper was substantial enough for two. He'll be hungry after travelling. Offer him a meal and talk to him.'

If only it were that simple. He'd probably prefer eating at the local pub to spending time with her. The last time she'd seen him, his parting remarks had been cold enough to cause Meg's pipes to freeze with no help from the weather.

Yet he hadn't sounded unfriendly on the phone. She cringed as she remembered teasing him about taking a jaunt to the Canary Islands. What had possessed her?

She'd imagined his smile as he'd replied, saying he could only cope with one crisis at a time. For a moment she'd forgotten they'd not parted friends. Her pulse had quickened as he told her he would be coming alone.

She had too much time to think as the hours ticked by. She checked the traffic reports, then went back to Meg's, for no other reason than to keep moving.

The devastation in her neighbour's previously cosy home seemed even worse now night was falling. Amy was distressed, aware that for the past few hours she'd been so distracted thinking about Mike that she'd almost forgotten why he was coming. Meg was going to be shattered by the damage.

Tonight would not be the time to tell Mike about Justin. It was a conversation for another day. For now, they needed to concentrate on sorting out Meg's home.

At last she heard his car. She pulled on her coat and went out to meet him. He looked tired and anxious. The urge to throw her arms around him was overwhelming, but she resisted as they went towards Meg's cottage. He opened the door, then turned to her.

'Thank you for calling me,' he said. 'I can manage now.'

Any warmth she had imagined in his voice had gone. He was polite, but that was all. It was obvious he didn't intend her to follow him indoors, but she ignored his hostility and trailed behind him as he took a quick look at the damage.

He went from room to room in complete silence, his face impassive. Amy knew she should go home, but wanted to help, if he'd let her.

'The kitchen's unusable,' she said. 'Would you like to come round to my cottage? I'll make coffee while you wait for the plumber. I've got food if you want a meal.'

He had been inspecting the plaster on the kitchen wall, but turned and glowered at her.

'What about the boyfriend? Won't he mind?'

'What boyfriend?'

'Don't pretend you don't know. The one with the flowers, the one … '

'He's not my boyfriend. He's not even a friend. I need to tell you about him. But … '

They were interrupted by a loud knock on the door.

'That'll be the plumber,' Mike said.

Amy left them talking and went home. If Mike was still angry after she'd explained, she'd accept it, but meanwhile she needed to be practical. She made a flask of tea and a plate of sandwiches and took them next door.

Both men were in the kitchen.

'I've left tea on the coffee table. Come and tell me what's happening later, Mike,' she called, and left before anyone could reply.

There was nothing more she could do.

It seemed ages, but in reality wasn't long before Mike came to return the flask and plate.

'Thanks for that,' he said. 'Henry ate most of the sandwiches. He's been working all day without a break. He's almost finished for now. He'll be back in the morning.'

'Do you want more tea?'

'Not now. I'd better go back and talk to Henry.'

He'd been avoiding eye contact as he spoke, looking somewhere over her shoulder at the wall, but as he turned to go he paused.

'I wanted to say I'm sorry I was so bad-tempered. I'd no right. You'd made it quite clear you weren't interested in me. What you do with your life, and who you're friends with, is none of my business...'

'Justin is not a friend,' Amy interrupted him.

He was speaking quickly, almost gab-

318

bling as he continued, almost as if he hadn't heard her. ' … and I'd like to eat dinner with you, if it's not too much trouble.'

She wasn't sure she'd heard him correctly.

'You want me to make dinner?'

At last he looked at her, and Amy saw her own misery reflected in his eyes.

'Or we could go out, if you prefer,' he said.

'My mother sent me home with enough food for a week. Come round when you're ready. I'll tell you about Justin while we eat.'

An hour later she heard the plumber's van drive off and started to heat the pie her mother had made. She set the table and waited, her heart thumping with trepidation. What would Mike's reaction be when he heard about her affair with a married man? A married man with young children. Would he believe she didn't know? That she'd been naive enough to believe Justin's lies?

When he eventually arrived, he was

carrying a bottle of wine.

'I found this in Aunt Meg's cupboard,' he said. 'I don't think she'll mind.'

Amy took the bottle from him and reached for wine glasses.

'Sit down,' she said. 'You're making me nervous, towering over me like that.'

Mike pulled out a chair and sat at the table. 'It's lovely and warm in here. It's going to be freezing next door until I can have the heating back on.'

'How long will that be?' she asked.

'Tomorrow, I hope. I'll talk to Henry in the morning.'

He chatted about the work that needed doing in Meg's cottage while she finished preparing the simple meal. He seemed to know she wasn't ready to talk yet. Her hands were shaking as she put the pie on the table and invited him to sit down.

'Could you pour the wine?' she asked, knowing she would be unable to manage without spilling it. 'I need a drink if I'm going to tell you about Justin.'

'You don't have to tell me anything,' he said, as he opened the bottle and filled her glass. 'Not if it's going to upset you.'

'But I do. You need to know why I kept pushing you away. Why I tried so hard not to fall in love with you.'

She took a gulp of her wine, struggling to find the words to go on, but it was Mike who spoke first.

'You tried not to fall in love with me?'

She nodded, miserably.

He pulled his chair close to hers and took her hand.

'Did you succeed?' he asked, so quietly she thought she had misheard. 'Did you succeed in not falling in love with me?'

The room was very quiet. She could hear the rain pattering on the window as she stared at her empty plate, intensely aware of his hand holding hers. His thumb was gently circling her palm. She could hear his steady breathing. But he made no attempt to move closer as he waited for her to reply.

She forced herself to look at him. His eyes were intent; gazing at her with so much love it was impossible to mistake it. She suspected he could read the same emotion on her own face. There was no point in trying to deny what was obvious.

'No,' she whispered.

He brushed her hair back from her face and leaned towards her, his warm breath caressing her skin as he spoke.

'Then you don't have to explain anything. Nothing else matters. I've loved you since the minute I saw you walking towards me, on the towpath across the aqueduct.'

His lips met hers in a gentle kiss, that became firmer as she ceased trying to suppress her feelings and reached her arms up to draw him closer. The meal remained uneaten. Having waited so long for that first kiss, neither wanted to draw apart.

It was Amy who broke away first.

'We need to talk.'

'Not about the past. You'll give me a list of reasons why I shouldn't love you. It's too late for that. Let's eat dinner and talk about our future.'

37

Amy returned the pie to the microwave to reheat. She was tempted to say nothing. He stood behind her, kissing the back of her neck, as she watched the timer count down. She leaned back against him and closed her eyes. The evening had become so special, why spoil it? She should do as Mike suggested. Look to the future.

The ping of the microwave jolted her back to reality. It would be so easy to ignore the past, but she didn't want to start this new relationship with any deceit. He'd been honest when he rushed off to rescue his ex. She needed to explain about hers. She returned the reheated cottage pie to the table, as Mike sat down.

'Help yourself,' she said.

He tucked in enthusiastically, but she toyed with her food. It was as if Justin were sitting at the table with them, his sardonic smile making the food taste like cardboard.

Lost in her thoughts, it was a while before she became aware that Mike had stopped eating, and was looking at her intently.

'What are you thinking about that's making you so sad?' he asked.

'Justin,' she admitted.

'The man who isn't a boyfriend, but brings you expensive flowers?'

She nodded, miserably.

'You know I love you,' he said. 'I think you love me. I was wrong to try to stop you telling me about him. He's making you unhappy — tell me why.'

'I met him when I started my first nursing post ... ' she began.

As she started to talk, it became easier. Mike didn't interrupt as she explained how they had met, how special he had made her feel, how dazzled she was by him.

'I thought I loved him,' she said. 'I was so wrong.'

She told him how Justin had wanted

to keep their romance a secret.

'Why?' Mike said. 'I want to tell everyone I love you. Especially Aunt Meg. She'll be so thrilled.'

'Not when she knows about Justin, she won't.'

'Why should she know about him? I was with Emma, you were with Justin. They're both past history.'

'Emma wasn't married,' Amy said. 'She didn't have young children. She wasn't living a lie.'

She couldn't look at him as she admitted her affair. She didn't hear him stand and come round the table. It was only when he cupped her chin in his hand, and raised her face to his, that she realised he was there.

Gently, he moved his thumb to wipe away the single tear rolling slowly down her cheek.

'Did you know he was married?'

'Of course not! His wife found out and phoned me. I was so ashamed. I've been ashamed ever since.' He pulled her into his arms.

'What did you have to be ashamed of? He deceived you.'

'His wife sounded lovely. She was sorry for me. That made it worse. She said it wasn't the first time he'd cheated on her, but it would be the last. When I told him I'd found out he was married, he threatened me. Said if I told his wife I'd be sorry.'

Mike was furious, and said so.

'I wasn't worried that he'd hurt me physically, but he could have started rumours about me and made my life very difficult. I never wanted to see or hear of him again. So I applied for a new job, in a new town.'

'Which is why you came to be renting a cottage in Hen Bont, and why we met. Love at first sight.'

'But I didn't accept it. After my experience with Justin I didn't want to risk loving again. I did everything I could to deny I was attracted to you.'

'What a lot of time we've wasted,' Mike sighed, as he bent his head to kiss her.

Amy lifted her arms to pull him closer, not wanting to let him go. She returned his kisses, finally accepting how much she loved him, and confident her love was returned.

'Was Justin the reason you reacted so strongly when you thought I was bullying Aunt Meg?' he said, when they finally drew apart.

Amy laughed as she returned to the table and belatedly began eating her food.

'I hadn't been able to forget you, though I'd tried; then, when we did meet again, you were shouting at Meg. I thought I'd judged badly again.'

Mike poured them both another glass of wine.

'You can't judge everyone by your experience with Justin.'

'I've realised that over the past few months. I've been so unhappy.'

'Has he been pestering you? You should have told me.'

Amy sipped at her wine.

'That was the first time I'd heard from

him since we split up. He'd just found out where I lived.'

'He wasn't threatening you, was he? I should never have driven off. I should have realised he was trouble and stayed to see you were all right.'

Amy smiled at him. 'Relax. He hadn't come to threaten me. Far from it. He told me his wife had found out about us, and she was divorcing him. He thought I would go back to him. I think he was recasting himself as the misunderstood husband who'd fallen in love with someone else. He chose to forget his lies, deceptions and threats.'

'What a nerve!'

'It was therapeutic to finally get the chance to tell him what I thought of him,' Amy said. 'I never want to think about him again.'

'Then don't.' Mike led her to the sofa and began distracting her with delicate kisses until she responded, pulling him closer and kissing him passionately, making up for all the miserable months.

★ ★ ★

Next morning the plumber arrived early. In daylight the damage to Meg's cottage looked even worse than it had the day before. The carpets downstairs were ruined. The bathroom and kitchen both needed to dry out, and their walls would need replastering. It would be some time before the place was habitable.

Mike rang the insurers, then Meg, while Amy went home to raid her mother's supplies for an early lunch.

It wasn't long before he came to tell her Henry had finished work, and the heating was back on.

'I can move the carpets and stack them outside to allow the place to start drying out,' he said, as they ate. 'I'll get on with that straight away.'

'What did Meg say?'

'She was more concerned with whether we were getting on all right than the state of her house. I told her we were getting on extremely well, thank you. She said to give you her love.'

Amy wanted to help him start moving the carpets, but Mike insisted she try to rest before her night shift. She didn't expect to sleep, but the past weeks of disturbed rest had left her exhausted. She closed her eyes, thinking of Mike's caresses, and woke several hours later. It was almost dark. She hurried next door to see how he was getting on.

He was stacking soaking wet rugs in the back yard. She picked her way through the mess to join him.

'Sleep well?' he asked, as he pulled her into his arms and kissed her.

Meg's back yard was almost as small as her own. It was dark, rain soaked and cold. But she was warm in his arms. When they eventually drew apart she saw a glimmer of white in the patch of soil near the wall. A cluster of tiny snowdrops had pushed their way through, their pure white petals glistening in the grey surroundings.

Mike leaned over to pick one, and handed it to her.

'I'm sorry it's not red roses,' he said.

330

She held the delicate flower in the palm of her hand. 'Snowdrops. The promise of spring.'

'The promise of a future life together,' Mike said huskily, as he led her back indoors and shut the door against the chill of the evening.

Meg's formerly cosy living room was a mess. The carpet was rolled up ready to be removed, the furniture was stacked in one corner, and everywhere smelt damp; yet it seemed the most romantic place she'd ever known as Mike held her close.

'I need to get ready for work,' she sighed, reluctantly pulling away.

'That's the story of our life,' Mike chuckled as he released her.

Amy was smiling as he walked to the door with her. This time, leaving him was different. This time she knew, when she returned, he would be waiting for her.

MURDER IN THE HAUNTED CASTLE

Ken Preston

Divorced Kim has come to terms with the fact that her only daughter is growing up. A last memorable holiday together before Maddie immerses herself in GCSE revision seems just the thing. But as if meeting the delectable James (no, not Bond — but close!) isn't exciting enough to throw a spanner in the works, just wait until they all get to the haunted castle. Dream holiday? More like a nightmare! But how will it end ... ?

ISLAND OF MISTS

Evelyn Orange

Arasay — remote Scottish island, wild-life haven, and home to Jenna's ancestors. When she arrives to help out her great aunt in the bookshop, she's running from her past and hiding from the world. But she's not expecting to meet an attractive wildlife photographer who is also using the island to escape from previous traumas. As Jenna embraces island life and becomes closer to Jake and his family, there are secrets in the mist that could threaten their future happiness …

ONE MAN'S LOSS

Valerie Holmes

Sir Christian Leigh-Bolton had never intended to gamble that night the vultures circled around Sir Howard. Losing heavily and in desperation, Sir Howard foolishly wagers away his inheritance, Kingsley Hall — and Christian steps in and wins the prize. Sir Howard's actions leave his sister, Eleanor, virtually homeless. Christian's honour is further tested when he makes a promise to Sir Howard, a dying man, not knowing if he can fulfil it. Meanwhile, Eleanor has taken matters into her own hands …

JESSIE'S LITTLE BOOKSHOP BY THE SEA

Kirsty Ferry

Jessie Tempest has two main interests: reading books and selling books. Her little bookshop in the seaside town of Staithes is Jessie's sanctuary from the outside world. When writer Miles Fareham and his inquisitive eight-year-old, Elijah, arrive to stay in the holiday apartment above the shop, it's testing – Jessie has always felt clueless around kids. But soon she realises that first impressions aren't always the right ones — and, of course, you can never judge a book by its cover!

AN OSCAR FOR EMMY

John Darley

Aspiring actress Emmy Fielding moves to Bishopston to escape her controlling boyfriend. Appearing in a popular TV medical soap, she meets fellow actor Oscar Timpson. They soon are attracted to one another, but their individual circumstances make a future together unlikely. Then, as they are about to star together in a production at the town's theatre, Emmy's boyfriend turns up. Emmy's confused. Who will she find happiness with — if anyone?